TIME DEPRESSED

By C. E. Chester

Tana,
   Its a rare and amazing thing
to find someone with book smarts
and common sense. I found one 25
years ago. I'm glad you found one, too.

C.E. Chester

I want to say thank you to Jonathan Burns for being the first to volunteer to help me, Mike Jeter for rereading this through every step of the writing process, and both of you for the great feedback you gave, even if you sometime gave the exact opposite advice. I would also like to express my gratitude to Tim Chester for the cover art.

CHAPTER ONE

Andrew Bower twisted the screw into the cork. He had taken off the jacket and tie he had worn to the office, but still wore his slacks and dress shirt. His sleeves were rolled up, as he opened the bottles of wine sitting on the table. His wife, Mimi, lit the candles. They both looked up when they heard the front door, but neither of them went to greet the house guest. The Thursday night dinners had started twenty years before when they were all balancing the time required to merge two companies and still spend time with their young families.

Stephanie was the first to arrive. She still wore the slacks and blouse she had worn to work in the lab. She said hi to Andrew, who she saw every day at the office, but hugged Mimi. They chatted for a moment about how their week had gone, but were interrupted by the chime on a cell phone.

"I just want to make sure this isn't anything important." Stephanie sat down in her normal seat to check it.

Heath and Elaine Radcliff were the next to arrive. They always seemed formal, even though the dinners were anything but. Heath said hello and then went immediately to his seat on the far side of the table. Elaine glanced at Stephanie, and saw that she was busy. So, she walked over to the hostess, both women squeezed hands, pressed cheeks together and then went to their seats.

Stephanie had her phone and purse put away when the

front door opened again. All the wine bottles were opened. All the food was in place. Monica Lane and Clint Bower rushed through the front door, sure they were late for dinner. When the couple got to the threshold of the dinning room, they saw two other seats still empty. Knowing they weren't the last to arrive, they stole a kiss before going in.

Andrew and Mimi Bower sat at each end of the long table. Since they had the large, formal dinning room and Mimi loved to cook, the majority of the dinners were served at their house. Clint sat down next to his mother, in the same seat he'd had since he required assistance cutting up his meat. Monica sat down between him and her mother, Stephanie. They both looked alike, other than the fact the mother had strawberry blond hair, while her daughter's was brunette. There was an empty chair between Stephanie and Andrew reserved for Rick Lane.

Across the table, Heath Radcliff sat alone with his wife, Elaine. There was an empty seat where their son, Jason, normally sat. They were the oldest couple at the table, and both sat with straight backs and their hands folded over the napkins in their laps waiting for dinner to officially start.

The clock in the hall chimed six times. Mimi looked across to her husband. "Is this everyone?"

"Jason is still in London," Monica replied.

"He'll be back tomorrow." Elaine added with a smile.

"Do you know where Rick is?" Heath asked Stephanie.

"I have no idea. I came here straight from the lab, and didn't see him when I left the office." She looked at her phone. "I don't have any messages from him."

"Should we wait until he gets here?" Mimi asked.

"Oh, no," Stephanie reassured everybody. "I'll send him a text message, but I'm sure he's just running late."

Everyone scooped food onto their plates from the serving dish that was closest to them, and then passed it clockwise down the table. The dinners were supposed to be casual, not that you could tell by looking. Most of them were wearing business attire, because they had come straight from work and hadn't bothered to change.

"The wine tonight is a new vintage I found last week. It should go great with the lamb chops."

Mimi ensured everything was done and the house staff left, so they could all feel comfortable talking without worrying about what was being overheard. Anything could be talked about at the table; business or personal. When the kids were little, there was always three bottles of wine on the table, so each adult could enjoy two glasses. Now, with everyone at the table being legal drinking age, there were four.

After pouring her glass, Elaine sniffed the bouquet. She closed her eyes as she drew in the fragrance. Her hand rocked gently, swirling the liquid inside the globe. Her eyes fluttered open as she took a sip. "Oh." She set the glass down. "That is good."

The hostess smiled, appreciating the positive feedback about her choice. Even though everything was arranged to be help yourself, she still watched to make sure everyone had enough. It was only after the others had started eating that she lifted her fork and joined them.

"Mimi and I have an announcement."

"Oh, Andrew."

"I know. I know. I should wait until the wedding, since it is a wedding present, but I can't." He turned to Clint and Monica. "Your mother and I have been talking, and we want to give you something that you'll think is as special as we think this union is. Something you will always cherish and remind you how great true love really is. It was simple when we thought about it. There is only one thing that does all that. So, on your wedding day, we are going to give you the lake house."

There was a moment of shocked silence.

"Does this mean we've seen the end of the company retreats?" Heath asked.

Everyone looked to Clint and Monica for the answer. They looked at each other, and stared into a mirror of their own expression. He sighed. She rolled her eyes.

"Of course not," Clint answered.

"Not unless we've lost our jobs." Monica added.

"Well, we are the newest employees," Clint joked around. "If layoffs are going to happen, we would be the first to be let go."

Andrew cleared his throat. All the kids knew that was a warning to stop goofing off.

The bride-to-be put down her fork and put her hands in her lap. "How do I explain this?" She paused and took a deep breath, while she figured out the best way to word what she wanted to say. "I've heard the story a hundred times. Heath and my Dad own a store front in Bozeman that sold traditional law enforcement equipment. Andrew owned a building here in Missoula where he developed state of the art less-than-lethal weapons. One night over drinks, the three of you decided to combine the old with the new."

"'It was never a family business,'" Clint said in a tone mocking the older men at the table.

Monica laughed. "Not even when I went to school and Mom started working in the lab. It wasn't having relatives working together that made this company into a family; it was the priority all of you put in making sure family came first."

"Thursday night dinners started out of necessity," Heath interjected. "The merger took up a lot of our time, and all three of you kids were all in diapers. The wives would have killed us if we didn't allow them some time of adult interactions."

"I understand everything was done in the most logical way, but my perspective is a little different that yours." Monica replied. "I grew up with everyone gathering at this table once a week. Anything and everything was open for discussion. One minute you guys would iron out business travel plans, and the next we would figure out what kind of dress I should get for the prom.

"For me." She looked over at her fiancé. "For us, there was no clear line where the company stopped, and our individual families began. There were Easter and summer breaks up at the lake. Which eventually lead to a satellite office and workshop up there. We were all a part of everything. I had an incredible childhood, where I knew anything I said was just as important as anything anyone else did. Other than the one year in high school I wanted to be an actress, I've never thought of doing anything else. We know all the big break-throughs for the company have happened up there. More gets done out on the deck with drinks that any staff meeting at the main office. We are all invested in seeing this company succeed, so we aren't going to stop the traditions that have been the most successful.

"Besides, our marriage brings two out of the three families together. We want to foster the feeling of this being a family company, not ruin that. I don't remember a Fourth of July that didn't have all of us up there, and I don't want to know what that would be like." She looked back and forth between her prospective in laws. "Thank you. I've loved that place since the first time I saw it. I will cherish it always."

Monica leaned into Clint and looked up into his brown eyes. She had a huge smile; one she seemed to wear all the time. It was reassuring to see he had the same goofy expression. Everything in her life seemed perfect and just when she thought she had everything, she got more. The only thing that would have made the moment better was if Jason was there to share it with them. He would be just as happy as they were.

"I know things are strained at the office. The wedding gives us all something to look forward to." Elaine said.

Everyone smiles and agreed with her assessment, and then went back to eating. The sound of silver ware clinking on China filled the room.

"Andrew, did you get my e-mail about the primers?" Stephanie asked. "I know you got a great deal on the last batch, but don't know who you got them through. I'm down to the last box, but there's no rush. I've ran the shotgun through ten thousand rounds. I'll be busy for at least a week seeing how it held up."

"I did. I was going to do it tomorrow. Since there is no

rush, I'll do a little shopping around and make sure I'm still getting the best price."

There was another break in the conversation. Mimi took a few more bites, waiting to make sure they were done before she spoke up. "The library has a fundraiser in July to raise money for the new building. I hoped Crown-n-Dale could be counted on to buy a table."

It was a formality for her to ask. She knew the company supported all her charities.

"Is this another black and white event?" Monica asked.

"No. You can wear color, but needs to be a dress. A very nice dress. If you need to go shopping, I'd be happy to take you," Mimi offered.

"I might have to take you up on that."

The hall clock chimed seven, and Elaine poured her second glass of wine. Monica noticed the older woman was always very proper. She would only have one drink per hour, always dressed impeccably, never had a hair out of place, and had perfectly straight posture. The younger woman tried to be like her, but felt like she fell a little short of the mark.

After dinner, Heath and Elaine were the first to excuse themselves. Andrew and Mimi settled into the living room. Stephanie stood in the hall, between the living room and the dinning room, looking at her cell phone.

"Did you hear from Dad?" Monica asked

"Not yet." The older woman shook her head. "I'm going to head home, incase he forgot it was Thursday, and is waiting there."

"Okay." Monica hugged her mother. "I'm going to help with clean up, so Clint doesn't have to do it all on his own."

"All right." Stephanie smiled. "If you lose track of time, just stay here. I don't want you out on the streets at two in the morning, even if it's just to come home."

"I love you, too."

Both women smiled at each other with a little tilt of their head. "It's been a long day. I'm probably going to bed early, so I won't see you until morning. Thank you for helping, and have a good night."

One more hug, and then Stephanie went down the hall to the front door. Monica watched her mother put on her coat and leave, then turned around and went back in the dinning room. She made a stack of dirty plates with silverware on top, and carried them into the kitchen. Clint was bent over opening the empty dishwasher, so they could load it.

"Nice ass."

Clint stood up and turned around. "You kiss your mother with that mouth?"

"Come to think of it, I just hugged her good bye. It must have been because I knew that profanity was in there just waiting to get out and I didn't want to soil her with it."

He laughed, and stepped out of the way so she could set her arm load in the sink.

"I'm beginning to think Jason intentionally plans these trips over Thursday night, just so he can get out of doing dishes," she said.

"I hadn't thought about it, but you might be right." He said before stepping out of the room. He returned with the plates still covered with food scraps and scrapped them into the trash can. "I don't think I could get away with it, but Jason seems to. Do you remember the time I told my Mom we should just leave the dishes for the maid, because she would be coming back in the morning?"

"How could I forget? That was the 'You don't know how good you've got it' speech. 'Most kids don't have hired help to pick up after them. They have to do the dishes every night.'"

"'All the dishes' Mom elaborated. 'Not just the plates and forks'. We never had to do the pots and the pans."

They both laughed as they continued to rinse off dishes and load them for washing. Clint brought in handfuls of stemmed wine glasses that all were run under the tap and then set on the top shelf.

"Did you ever make that mistake again?" Monica set a

plate she had just rinsed off on to the rack and took the one Clint held out for her.

"Are you kidding me? Mom said if she ever heard another comment like that, she was going to instruct the house cleaner to not touch my bedroom or bathroom. The fear of scrubbing soap scum was enough to keep me in line."

Three chords rang out. Monica dried her hands and then pulled out her cell phone. "Jason texted. He offers his congratulations on our wedding gift. I'm messaging him back: OMG. Can you believe it?"

Clint went back to the dinning room. He set the dishes he brought back out of her reach. "We don't have to wash these. They weren't used." He put them back into the cupboard as she looked at the next message on her phone.

"He's worried were going to turn the lake house into our love nest and not let anyone else come back up."

"Tell him to stop being absurd."

"Okay." Monica typed the message. "I also added that he will always have a bedroom there, because it wouldn't be home without him."

Clint took over rinsing the last couple dishes as she continued corresponding.

"I asked how everything was going."

There was a long pause until the phone chimed again, during which Clint got the last few dishes loaded up. He went back out to the dining room, and came back with a wine bottle in hand.

"It doesn't sound like things went well for him," she said while looking down at her phone and then looked up to see him taking a swig straight from the bottle. "What are you doing?"

"There's a little left in this bottle, and all the glasses are already rinsed. I didn't want to have to wash another."

She took the bottle from him and poured the last little bit into her mouth. "Jason said he did everything he could. I told him that's all we ask. We'll see him in the office tomorrow to get a full report."

Clint took the bottle from her, put it in the trash can beside them, pulled her into a hug and kissed her.

CHAPTER TWO

"Good Morning." Monica was her normally cheerful self as she stepped into the office of Heath Radcliff.

"Are you actually getting some work done today? I thought you'd be completely caught up in wedding plans."

She knew he was teasing her, but underneath that he did disapprove of anything that interfered with work. "As a woman, I am able to multitask. I can get my work done, and take time out of my day to shop for a dress with the Moms."

"Studies have shown that all multitasking does is decrease your proficiency in each individual task."

"Then let's stop talking about this, and focus on work."

She plopped down in the chair across from him. He leaned back with a sigh and folded his hands across his lap. He looked out the window, over her shoulder. She knew he was formulating what he wanted to say.

"Not getting those government contracts really hurt us."

Monica paused, waiting for the rest of his comment. That was a pretty simple statement, not one he would have to put a lot of thought into. When he didn't say anything more, she finally responded. "I know we invested a lot of time, effort, and money into getting those. The last few years have been filled with product development and long hours of reading and re-reading the what the government wants."

"Apparently, we 'invested' our money the wrong way. We should have been buying politicians."

With a frown, she responded, "I know that's how our competition landed the contacts. The problem is they don't have the goods. We are the ones with a lab filled with state of the art equipment. We just need to wait them out. According to the contract, they have one year to hand over working prototypes. When they can't deliver..."

"They will get an extension."

She sighed. "More time won't give them the technology. Eventually, they will have to admit they can't produce the goods, and that's when we will step in."

"And just hope we don't go bankrupt in the meantime."

The old man had a tendency to hold onto an opinion once it was it was formed. She had seen this stubborn streak in him before. But this wasn't something she was going to give in on.

"Jason is out drumming up business overseas. We need to go talk to police chiefs and get in touch with private agencies."

"This is going to be a nightmare, a very expensive, time consuming nightmare."

"That might be, but we've already learned the hard way we can't put all our eggs into one basket. It might take a hundred baskets to match the one we lost, but that just means losing one customer won't be a devastating loss."

"I should have stuck with my original business, and not gotten caught up in this merger?"

"And you'd still be back in Bozeman selling expandable batons. You need to trust us. I've made a list of every city in the U.S. that has had a riot in the last ten years. The list is fairly long. We are going to get in touch with every police chief in each of those cities and let him or her know we have a better way to protect their people and officers."

"All right," he said. "You've worn me down. What can I do?"

"I'm making a catalog of every product we have put through testing. I need to know prices for everything. I need an amount to list in the catalog, and I also need to know the minimum we can charge without losing money."

Monica scanned her ID and the door to the laboratory opened. She stepped through, and waited for it to close. The security protocol to ensure no one else entered with her was second nature. All four walls had stainless steel countertops and cupboards with glass doors. Personal Protective Equipment covered the wall to her right, and there was a bullet trap in the far corner. Double hearing protection was required for everyone in the room whenever that was used.

Stephanie stood with her back towards the door, looking into a microscope. A new bean-bag launcher laid disassembled on the counter, and the microscope was being used to look for any stress fractures in the plastic parts after ten thousand rounds had been fired.

"Mom, did you forget what today is?"

"Of course not." The older woman turned, stretching her neck as she stood up straight. "I set an alarm so I wouldn't lose track of time."

As she reached for the cell phone on the counter, it started chiming.

"See, you're early."

Stephanie took off her lab coat, revealing the floral dress she wore underneath. It wasn't the kind of thing her mother usually wore to work, so she had remembered their plans.

"I was just trying to keep busy."

"What's going on?" Monica was concerned. Her mother couldn't keep still when she worried.

"You're father not only missed dinner, he didn't come home last night."

"That's not like him," the daughter admitted. "but we've all been under a lot of stress here. I bet he's concocted some great plan to save us all, and is out putting it all together so he can come sweeping back into town the big hero."

"You're probably right." The mother slipped her phone into her purse and put the strap over her shoulder. "That man eats, sleeps and breathes, to make a profit. He'll have figured something out."

Mimi and Elaine were waiting for them when the stepped into the lobby. They all hugged. Monica thought Mimi's was really tight and held for a few seconds after what seemed like a natural point for the embrace to end. Elaine's was stiff and over as quickly as it began.

"I've been kind of busy, so I haven't had time to look at the reviews of the dress shops."

"You don't have to worry about that," Elaine said. "I know all the best places, and I've already told the driver where to go."

❖ ❖ ❖

Clint's office door was open. Monica walked through, said "Good afternoon", and closed the door behind her.

"Oh, hey" He looked up from his computer. "How was shopping?"

"Tedious, at first." She plopped down on the couch. "But it got better. The Moms talked me into spending more than I planned to."

He got up and joined her on the other side of the room. "I assume that means you found one you liked."

"Yes." She smiled. "It's amazing. I didn't think I would be into all this frilly stuff, but they had one dress that was just gorgeous. And it looks great on me. I do kind of look like one of those little cake toppers in it, but it's so elegant."

"I can see why they convinced you to buy it. You light up just talking about it." He pulled her into his arms and whispered in her ear. "I can't wait to see you in it."

"You aren't seeing it until I walk down the aisle." She turned her head to he could see how serious she was.

"That's what I meant." He smiled and pulled her onto his

lap.

The door opened, and Jason swaggered in. He wore no tie, and the top button on his shirt was undone. His hair, normally pulled back, hung loosely around his shoulders. He sat down in the chair opposite them. "You two should get a room."

"We had one," Clint responded. "A nice private one you barged into without knocking."

"It doesn't seem very private, now." Jason leaned back.

"How was London?" Monica asked, sliding off her fiancé's lap, but staying close enough to remain in contact with him.

"Cold and rainy. Overall, it was a dreary two weeks. Scotland Yard is very interested in our products. They are always looking for ways to minimize injuries and casualties during riots. The problem is that there isn't any money in the budget for new equipment. I don't think the government will give them the money until a bad lawsuit happens and they realize it would have been cheaper if they would have just bought our stuff to begin with."

"Well, keep with it." Clint responded. The clock on the wall chimed four times. They all sat in silence until it was finished "Once in a while a politician will pull their head out of their ass and do the right thing before the shit hits the fan."

"We're going to the lake house tonight," she said. "You coming up?"

Rolling his eyes, Jason replied: "You guys are June and Ward Cleaver. By eight o'clock you'll be in your flannel pajamas, sitting on either side of the fireplace, reading before you go to bed."

"Sound great."

"What's wrong with that?"

Jason walked over to the window and motioned to the city beyond it. "You guys are missing out on the prime of your lives. I've been all over the world, and nothing I've seen competes with the night life right here, in Missoula. Tonight, there are four different concerts playing. Not to mention the breweries, dance clubs and assortment of other bars just in the downtown area. But instead of going out and enjoying yourselves, you run off to the country and hide from civilization."

"You should come up and bring civilization to us."

"I can't tonight." Jason sat back down. "I have a date. I'll be up tomorrow around one."

"You have a date?" Monica asked.

"Yes."

"Is it with anyone we know?"

"I'm not aware of it if introductions have been made."

"When do we get to meet her?"

"You don't," Jason replied

"Why not?"

"Because it's not that kind of relationship."

That comment made the other's stop and think, giving a lull in the otherwise fast conversation.

"But you've seen her more than once?"

"Yes."

"I think we should at least know who she is," Monica persisted.

"You don't understand. It's just physical. Outside of that, we don't interact. If I ever find a relationship," He made quotation marks with his fingers. "you'll be the first to know."

Clint and Monica looked at each other, but didn't say anything.

"Other than the big announcement of the wedding present at dinner last night, was there anything unusual going on."

"Nope."

The intercom buzzed, and Andrews voice came through. "Is Monica with you?"

Clint walked over and pressed the button to talk. "Yeah, she's right here."

"How about Jason? Do you know where he is?"

"I'm here, too," he said loud enough for the microphone to pick up. "What's going on?"

"I need all of you to come down to the lab. Right now."

"Sure. Why?" Clint asked.

"I'll explain when you get down here."

Then a click indicated the connection had been dropped. All three of them looked at each other, but they all had the same bewildered expression. They all shrugged, got up, and headed out the door and to the stairs.

CHAPTER THREE

The door to the lab was standing open when they got down there. It was their first indication something was seriously wrong. The door was always kept locked, and each person had to scan their identification to get in and out. Why were those security measures suddenly being bypassed?

Andrew, Stephanie and Heath were waiting inside. Everything looked the same as it had that morning; exactly the same. It seems no progress had been made in the search for microscopic fractures. Heath stepped aside revealing the vault door was open.

"What's going on?" Clint asked.

"Why is the vault empty?" Monica asked

Clint and Jason both turned to the open door and saw the empty shelves inside. Monica's eyes shot to her mother; the person that spent the most time in the lab. Heath was the first one to speak up.

"While you guys were out shopping, I came down here to find out how many of the Skunk Grenades we had. I found it empty, of everything. I immediately checked out the security system. Everything was locked, and no alarms had been triggered. So, I pulled up the log to see who had been the last person in here. The vault was opened last night at six pm, by Rick Lane."

"While we were at dinner?" Clint asked.

"Yes. The vault was open for forty-three minutes. Six minutes later he left the building. Security cameras show him exiting with two large suitcases. He loaded both into the back of his SUV, and drove away."

There was a moment of silence while that was absorbed.

"Why would he take all of it?" Monica wondered out loud.

"We don't know." Heath answered.

"Where did he go?" Jason questioned.

By the blank looks, it seemed no one had an answer to that.

"I found a confirmation for two plane tickets, one in Rick's name and one for the receptionist. The flight left Sacramento two hours ago, headed to Mexico City."

"Well, I guess I don't have to finish that personnel file entry for her missing work today without calling out," Clint said.

That earned him a frown.

"Sacramento?" Monica spoke next. "That can't be a coincidence. He took all of our top-secret prototypes, and then flew out of the city where our competition is located."

"I didn't want to hire that woman." Heath said. "I thought she was a corporate spy. Rick just laughed at me. I wonder if this was all set up last year? Stephanie, did you know how long this might have been happening?"

"I assumed he was sleeping with her. He did with most of the office women, and his personal trainer." She spoke without emotion, but looked down when she saw the sympathy from everyone.

"Why would he go to Mexico City?"

"I don't think that was his final destination. We went to South America two years ago. It was the first time he took interest in something outside of work. He commented on how cheap it would be to live down there."

Andrew cleared his throat. "A couple hours ago, I got a call from a friend of mine in Congress. He said I must have been mistaken about ProTech's capabilities, because they had scheduled a meeting with the oversight committee to show off what they have next month."

"He sold it to them?" Clint said with disbelief.

"It looks that way." Heath answered.

"Did you call the cops?" Jason asked.

"They left a few minutes ago. They filled their reports. They didn't sound optimistic about being able to do anything." Stephanie said.

"Did you call our lawyer?"

Andrew piped up. "I spoke with Walter as soon as we realized what had happened. He said we might not be able to go after ProTech; they bought the products from one of the CEOs of our company. Our only recourse might be to go after Rick."

"If we can find him." Heath added with a frown.

"Won't our patents protect us?"

"They are supposed to." Andrew replied. "Many times, in history, the honest man gets screwed over by large corporations, especially when they have a politician in their pocket. It's strange how fuzzy the law gets when government officials get involved."

"What are we supposed to do?" Monica asked.

"There is not much we can do tonight." Heath answered. "Go home. Eat. Rest. Just get over the shock of it. Tomorrow we will come in ready to tackle this."

Monica was in a daze as she walked back up stairs. She could hear Clint's footsteps as he followed, but her mind was in too much turmoil to really focus on it. How could her father have betrayed her like that? She would admit that she had never really been that close to him, but that didn't mean he could abandon her and take everything she had. Jason was not close to his father, but that didn't mean he would sell him out. That had been the magic of their childhood; they had all had three sets of parents, and there had never been any pressure to be closer to one set, just because they were the biological parents. She couldn't help but wonder if that assumption had been a huge mistake. If she had been a dutiful daughter would it have kept all this from happening?

Even though the idea seemed preposterous, she couldn't help but consider it. Her father did not have the knack for numbers like she did. If she had only learned what he did for the company, her greatest gift would have gone unused. Without her mathematical equations to prove the theories correct, they wouldn't have been able to come up many of their new inventions. She knew the company had been a team effort, and she had been a key component. If she had been acquiescent, only taking the same steps her father had, they wouldn't have had many of their recent break-throughs.

She stepped through her office door, and heard Clint close it behind her. She just stood there, realizing she had no idea what to do next. She always had something on her list of things to accomplish, but all the stuff that had seemed so important suddenly did not matter anymore. She turned around, not seeing anything in the room. When her eyes finally did settle on something, it was the white plastic bag hanging from the coat hook. Tears filled her eyes. She stepped around her fiancé and unzipped the bag.

"What are you doing? I'm not supposed to see that?"

"What difference does it make, now. I don't get to keep it." When the front gaped open, she pulled out handfuls of the silky material. She remembered how it looked in the three-hundred-and-sixty-degree mirror. The straps were about an inch wide, coming down to a neck line that revealed just enough. The waistline was form fitting, but from there flowed down and ended with an edge that looked like ribbon. The two-inch-wide ribbon like fabric cascaded down from her knees to her ankles. It was the most beautiful dress she had ever seen "I didn't think we could afford it this morning, now I know we can't."

She swallowed a lump in her throat. "That is, if you even want to marry me, anymore?"

He took her by the shoulder, and made her face him. "Why would I think that?"

"My father just ruined your entire life."

"You have been just as affected by his actions as I have been." He lifted her chin until she met his eyes. "What happened doesn't change my feelings for you, at all. I was worried that you would want to call off the wedding, now that I might not be the CEO of your favorite company anymore."

"Don't say that." She buried her face in his shirt. "I can't give up hope yet."

CHAPTER FOUR

From the outside, the building looked the same. The bright morning sunshine reflected off the front, just like it did every sunny morning. Clint and Monica held hands, content to stand with the Expressway traffic at their backs, and not actually go in.

"Hey, you two." Jason walked up, putting an arm over each of them. "Do you know why we've all been called in so early?"

"It was your Dad that called, we figured you would know."

"He just told me to be here. I didn't know he was the one behind the orders, I thought they might have come from Andrew."

"Nope, we are in the dark as much as you are."

They all stood there, staring at the door. None of them made the first move to go inside. The building looked peaceful from where they stood, but none of them expected that tranquility to continue once they stepped over the threshold.

"Well?" Jason asked. When no one responded, he continued. "We might as well find out what the plan is."

Monica turned to her friend. "Do you really think there is a way to fix this?"

"There is only one way to find out."

With a slight nudge, they all started walking forward. Clint held open the door, and then followed the other two inside. Elaine sat behind the receptionist desk.

"Mom, what are you doing here?"

"Someone had to sit at this desk." She tapped a pen on the notepad in front of her. "Your father assures me that I will only be here for a few days. I would much rather be at hot yoga."

"We appreciate you being here," Monica said.

The older woman smiled in response, but didn't say anything. They all stood there in the silence, politely smiling.

"Something's different," Clint commented.

They all looked around the room. None of the furniture had been moved. The plants were sitting in the same spot by the window. The lights were all on.

"The music isn't playing." Jason said.

All three of them looked at the woman sitting behind the receptionist desk. She was staring at the computer screen, and didn't notice. She clicked the mouse, and the familiar sound of a computer simulated deck of cards shuffling came from the computer. Jason smiled at the realization his mother was playing solitaire.

"I'll get it." The younger Radcliff walked around the desk, squeezed behind his mother, and flipped the stereo on. Instantly, music flowed down from speakers all over the building. Once he was back on the other side of the furniture, he asked "Where's the old man?"

"He's in the back."

Elaine went back to her game, oblivious to the confused look on the other's faces. 'The back' was not how they described any part of the building. Did she mean back in his office? Maybe he was back in the break room. A noise saved them from having to ask; he was in the assembly area.

Heath stood at a white board making a list. He turned around when he heard the door, put down the marker and crossed his arms.

"Good. You're here. I'm going to need all hands for the next couple of days. We are going to be in a legal battle over the patent, and the scrimmage starts today. We have four orders for our products, and we need to fill them. Having items sold will

27

concrete our position as patent holders. I know all the finished products were taken, but we still have parts. I want all the replacements made and shipped out ASAP, hopefully before Pro-Tech even announces they have our equipment. Just having the patent should protect us, but we don't live in a perfect world. We need to cover all of our bases, and, more importantly, we need to get some income rolling in."

Stephanie came up the back stairs carrying a box. "I got everything we'll need from the lab."

Everyone gathered around to see the assortment of parts in the box. One by one, they each took something out of the box and set it on the table. All that was in it was miscellaneous parts and tools they would need. Once the box was empty, and stored on the shelf underneath, the excitement was over.

Heath pointed at the white board. "That's the list of everything we need to make Stephanie. I want Jason and you to make sure we have all the parts to make thirty Flash Shields. That's how many we've already sold, so we need at least that much. Make a list of everything we are short on."

Flash Shield was trademarked by their company for the new riot shields they had designed. Imbedded in the front of the armor was a light. It pulsated in a sequence that irritated the human optic nerve, leaving people unable to focus on it. Being unable to look at the shield, and whoever it defended, meant people would also be unable to aim at it. Just another level of protection to whomever was behind it.

"Clint and Monica, you'll be on the Tracker Rounds. Police chiefs aren't sure their people can shoot a moving vehicle, and get the GPS tracker to stick, so we've only sold twenty-four. I'm sure once they're used in the field, word will get out, and sales will go up. So, we need to get that ball rolling."

"Did I hear last night we we're out of primers?" Clint asked.

"We are almost out of shotgun primers," Stephanie clarified. "We have a box of one thousand of the primers used for those rounds."

"I'm going to work on the Skunk Grenades at the back bench. Any questions?"

Everyone shook their head. Just when they were about to split up, the back door opened. Mimi walked in with a box, and set it down on the clear end of the table they were all gathered at. They could smell the baked bread before they even looked inside.

"Bagels and cream cheese," Mrs. Bower said. "I've got coffee and fruit in the car. I'm sure you boys wouldn't mind grabbing that for me."

Jason and Clint headed towards the door.

"We're here to work, not to have a picnic," Heath griped.

Mimi turned to him with a smile. "We are here to work. We'll get a lot more done on full stomachs. My father always said well-fed workers are happy workers."

Heath grumbled something under his breath, but didn't argue any more. Mimi sat out all the food and flatware, so it would be easy for everyone to get what they needed.

"When is Andrew going to get here?"

"He's not."

Mimi set the last bagel on the plate, wiped her hands off with a napkin, and turned her full attention to the older man. His scowl had turned into blatant shock.

"What do you mean he's not coming in? This is a crisis. We need everyone here if we are going to get through this."

"He's just as upset about this as you are." Mrs. Bower responded. "He had to have a cognac to get to sleep, and still only got a few hours of rest. His brain is going a million miles an hour, and isn't going to stop."

"So, where is he?"

"I told him to go to the lake house."

"What?" Heath yelled. "Everything's falling apart, and you send him up for a relaxing weekend?"

"You know as well as I do that man never relaxes. Who else has an office and a workshop at their vacation home? I've been married to him a long time, and I can tell you, keeping him here would have been a big mistake. He needs space to let whatever ideas he has come to fruition. Being here." Mimi motioned to the room around them. "Impersonating a factory worker, will only kill any inspiration he has right now. I told him to go. I'm here instead to do whatever manual labor you need."

"You send one of the most brilliant minds away, and you think you're going to take his place?"

"Wow, that's the closest you've come to insulting me. I'm not stupid. In fact, I'm smart enough to know this room is already filled with all the brain power we need. All we are doing is assembling parts, and the five of you have been involved with this since these products were just concepts. So, if there is anything that doesn't bolt right into place, we have the know how right here to fix it. You don't require another engineer. All you need is a monkey to turn a wrench."

"Um, Mimi," Stephanie interrupted. "We could use you're help over here. When these parts come out of the molds, the edges aren't clean. Sometimes that little extra bit of plastic can keep the pieces from snapping together. Can you grind these down, so they are all smooth?"

The founder's wife put of a pair of safety glasses, slid on gloves, picked up the rotary tool, and went to work. Everyone else sorted through boxes, inventorying what they had and making a list of what they needed. Heath finally gave up scowling at everyone's backs and went to his own work area.

CHAPTER FIVE

Andrew stood next to the work bench with both hands flat on it's surface. His head hung down below his shoulders, in defeat. He had left the city determined to come up with a new product to sell; one ProTech did not have.

He had locked himself in his shop, since that was where most of the great ideas had come from. That was why they called it the 'think tank' after all. He just wanted one new item, just to show everyone that they hadn't been beat.

After two days of pacing, staring at the walls, and slewing strings of profanity, nothing had come to him. He had tried laying out miscellaneous parts on the bench in front of him, hoping his brain would come up with a novel way to put them together. After an hour of staring at them with no ideas, he rearranged the pieces hoping it would help. He looked at them for another hour without any epiphanies. After that, the parts went flying with a sweep of his arm.

That is what led to him leaning on the table with his head hung down. His company was supposed to be his great achievement, a legacy that was being passed down to his son. It was more than just his son. After two decades of them hanging around, Monica and Jason were like his children, too. The weight on his shoulders was tripled because all of them were being let down.

There was a knock at the door. After a deep breath, he pushed himself off the bench top. He figured the others had tracked him down. He had hoped he would have something to show them before he'd have to face them again. To his surprise, when he opened the door, it was the cook standing there.

"You barely touched your dinner last night, left without eating breakfast this morning, and didn't come back for lunch. If you're going to put in long hours out here, you need to give yourself the fuel to sustain you."

"You're right. The brain doesn't have any nutritional stores, like muscle tissue does. It is the first thing effected by drops in the blood sugar levels."

"Exactly." Tess handed over the picnic basket. As soon as he had a firm grasp on it, she turned around and headed back towards the parking lot.

"Thank you, Tess."

With a quick wave, she was in her car and driving away. He carried the food inside and sat down at the desk. The first item he pulled out of the basket was a thermos. The smell of tomato soup greeted him when he opened it. Did she really make his favorite? He felt around, and then pulled out a napkin folded around something square. He unwrapped it to see that there was a grilled cheese sandwich inside. It was still warm. He bit into it and moaned when he tasted that it had been made with sour dough bread and not the multi-grain his wife had switched them to.

Instantly, his stomach came to life with the hunger he had been ignoring. He was drinking the soup straight from the thermos, and made himself stop and take a deep breath. He forced himself to slow down and enjoy the meal, rather than devour it to fill his empty stomach.

After savoring each bite of the sandwich, and then turning the thermos upside down to get the last drop of soup, he reached back inside the basket and found an apple, a bottle of water, and two brownies. He really needed to give Tess a raise. Hopefully he would find a way to get the money, so he could.

He leaned back in his chair and bit into the baked chocolate. The familiar taste filled him with memories of a simpler time. Everyone had always said what a genius he was. Even from a young age, he had been told he was destined for greatness; the only thing holding him back was his own imagination. He felt like not only was he letting his colleagues down with this business failure, but he was being let down by all those people that had built him up so high.

The very land he was sitting on was a perfect example of how out of control he had allowed his dreams to get. He had bought it because there was an old mine on the back of the property that went deep into a mountain mainly consisting of quartz. He had remembered, back in college, learning about how paramagnetic drew in the electromagnetic field and diamagnet repelled it. If that were the case, then space-time wouldn't be able to penetrate things like bismuth, antimony, and quartz. His young mind leaped to the next step; if he made an artificial electromagnetic field deep inside the Earth rich in one of those elements he would create a separate space-time continuum that could move faster or slower that the one on the surface.

He had even done sketches of what he thought the machine would look like. He turned his chair around and opened the bottom drawer of the file cabinet. He found the papers hanging in the folder at the very back. All the pages were still there; a detailed drawing and a list of everything he needed to fabricate it. He never had the nerve to build it.

He laid the pages out on the desk. The diagram in front of him sparked the memories from when he had first penned it. In all the excitement of imagining himself being the first person to create a time machine, there was a fear of causing a time paradox and potentially destroying everything.

Suddenly all those past fears didn't seem so dire. When he had made the drawings, he didn't have a need for a time machine. Everything in his life had been just fine. Now, not so much. After two days of pacing in the shop without a single idea, his past concerns about changing the timeline didn't seem so bad.

His finger tapped on the edge of the desk. There was one major component not on the papers. He needed a computer software program to run the machine. Twenty-eight years ago, he didn't have that skill set. Time had corrected that. He opened the laptop and started working.

Andrew stood at the entrance to the mine, wishing it was just a little bigger. If it were just a few feet higher and wider, he could build the machine in the shop, and then take it down. Instead, he had to take everything down in pieces, along with all the tools he would need to convert the cavern into a makeshift workshop.

He pulled a lawn and garden wagon. It was the best option the store had, even if he felt silly pulling it. He knew, without it, he would have to carry everything down one arm load at a time. Why couldn't he have bought a mine with railroad tracks?

"Hi ho, hi ho, it's off to work I go."

As he sang, Bower flipped on the light on his helmet and headed into the mine. This was the last load; tools and miscellaneous gear he thought of at the last moment. It was much lighter and less cumbersome than the other ones had been. The path he followed down the tunnel had thick electrical cords running down both sides of it. They led to a newly installed work lights that glowed far ahead of him.

In the two dozen trips he had made into the ground, he had worn a fairly clean path. Which was a good thing, since his mind was on the details of the schematics and not where his feet were landing. He had twelve pieces of steel that were three inches wide and a half inch thick. They had been pre-bent into an arc. Four of the pieces were six feet long, four of them were two inches shorter than that, and the last four were another two inches shorter. He used a welder to connect all the pieces of the same length, until he had three circles laying on the ground inside the other.

Once those were done, he built the base to support it all. He had to use a winch mounted to the scaffolding that supported the work lights to hold the weight while he put all the pieces together. He didn't stop until a twenty-four-foot sphere stood in front of him. The small of his back ached from staying in one position for extended periods of time. His clothes were filthy and potted with burns. Looking up at the structure, he felt good about what he had accomplished in one work day.

On his way out of the mine, he turned off the fans he had installed as he passed them. The last one was just a few feet from the entrance. He had expected bright light outside, and was surprised to see it dark. After stepping clear of the rock tunnel, he looked up at the moon still partially blocked by the tree tops. He hadn't planned on working that late, but was too excited about the progress he was making to stop.

He drove back to the lake house, thinking about all the work he had planned for the next day. The magnets needed to be attached. There was, what seemed like, miles of wires to lay out. He looked forward to when all the assembly was complete, and he could start the tests.

Squinting into the glare, Andrew vowed it would be the last time. He stood at the make shift work table he had set up in the mine. He had tried four different spots on the bench, and all of them had a work light shining in his eyes. He walked across the cavern and angled the bulb away from where he sat. He went back to his seat, and sighed in relief. He could finally clearly see the computer screen, and could concentrate on his work.

Everything was set up. The batteries had a full charge. It was time for him to find out if this was going to work or not. He set a fish in a bowl on the platform designed for him to stand on. He had to ensure that the trip wouldn't be fatal. Then he would make sure it would carry him.

He confirmed the power going to all three magnets were

positive, not negative. All the fittings were secure. He slid the machine out to the center of the room, in the area he had marked off with tape. He could imagine the time machine going through time, and landing where the machine from that time was already parked. That was when he got out the tape and marked out a launching zone.

Once that was done, he logged into the laptop. Its batteries were fully charged. He pulled up the program and entered in that he wanted three percent power for fifteen seconds. He had a stop watch in his left hand and his right hand on the mouse. He clicked the start icon.

He stepped back, getting as far away from the device as he could. The magnets spun along the track. Everything slid smoothly without sparks or unexpected noises. The magnets continued to spin for the full time, and then came to a stop.

He looked down at the unused stopwatch in his hand. His plan was to time how long the machine disappeared, but it hadn't vanished from sight. He let out a pent-up breath, and tried to think of things in a different perspective. There hadn't been any smoke or fire. It was nice to know the electromagnetic rail system worked. But he had expected something... else. Anything to indicate the contrivance had traveled through time.

He looked down at the watch on his wrist. It read the same time as the computer screen; one minute after he started the magnets. Could the experiment have affected everything in the mine, and not just inside the rails? He didn't think that could be the case, but he needed to know for sure.

Safety first. He disconnected all the batteries and shut down the computer. He also pushed the machine back into its normal spot in the corner. When that was done he turned off all the work lights. With a flashlight to show him the way, he headed for the surface.

There was a clock just inside the shop. It read the same time as his watch. Well, that proved he had not moved through time. What he had done was waste twenty minutes hiking out of the mine. Well, maybe he had learned something. The rail system worked. None of the magnets had jammed. In reality, it had gone very smoothly. Now, he just had to figure out why the magnetic field hadn't caused time to change.

He did the test again, setting up everything just as he had the first time. The batteries were still at ninety-eight percent, so he didn't have recharge them. This time he set it up to run at five percent for half a minute. He clicked the mouse, and started backwards. It only made it three feet and fell on his ass. The iron structure in front of him disappeared, startling him and making him lose his balance. He quickly pressed the start button on the timer. He scurried backwards until his back hit rock, never taking his eyes off the center on the room. He had done it. He made a machine that traveled through time.

He sat there on the ground staring at an empty space. Eventually curiosity made him look down at the stopwatch. Two minutes had passed, and the seconds were climbing. He had no idea how long before it would reappear. He assumed the small amount of energy he had applied wouldn't propel it more than a few minutes. He just had to patiently wait.

Finally, it appeared just as quietly and suddenly as it had disappeared. His thumb ceased the time adding to the stopwatch. He looked down and saw ten minutes and forty-three seconds on the screen.

It worked. He did it. He made a machine that could travel through time. The test had gone really close to what he expected it to. Even from where he sat, he could see the betta fish swimming around in a circle, just like he had before the trip. Now, all he had to do was reverse everything and see if it went back in time. Then repeat the test over and over with different power and time until he had a predictable system to know how long the trip would be.

CHAPTER SIX

Monica sat in the passenger seat of her mother's car. She tipped her bottle of water up, and drank the last of it. After putting the cap back on, she tossed it into the back seat. When she heard the bottle hit something, she turned around to see what it was.

"What's in the box?"

"It's all the stuff from your father and my trip to South America. I wanted to burn it all, but Heath said to give it to the private investigator. I told him it was just a bunch of souvenirs and crap, but they want anything that might point them in the right direction."

Stephanie pushed down on the turn signal, steered into the left turn lane, and pulled up to the red light. When the car was stopped, she looked over at her daughter. The younger woman looked straight ahead.

"So, they are really trying to find him?"

The turn arrow turned green. A quick glance showed her daughter still didn't look at her.

"Only to make him pay for what he did. Nobody wants him back."

Monica looked over at her Mom as they pulled into the parking lot. "I've always felt like Dad wasn't really involved in my life. He was there, but he really wasn't a part of it. I never realized you felt the same way."

"Oh, sweetie. I tried to do everything I could to give you a good childhood."

"You succeeded. I love my life. I never thought about it until he left. Dad was always around, but looking back, I realize we rarely interacted. If I needed help, I came to you, or Andrew, or Heath. It was nothing against Dad, I went to the person that had the answers I needed. Dad was in sales, which I never took an interest in. Realizing your relationship with him was the same is sad. I assumed you had a private connection with him I didn't see, but if he was sleeping around on you I don't think that can be the case. Were you ever happy with him?"

Stephanie took the keys out of the ignition and put them in her purse. The purse sat in her lap. She closed her eyes and leaned back against the head rest.

"When I met your father, he was like the leading man in a classic movie. He didn't have to say anything; he just gave me a look, a kiss, and swept me off my feet. He was going to take on the world, and I couldn't believe I was the one he wanted by his side while he did it. The next thing I knew, I was a wife. And then a mother. It was like being caught up in a whirlwind. It was years before I got my bearings and realized by life hadn't turned out how I wanted it to."

Monica reached over and touched her mother's hand. "Well, then there is one good thing in all this. At least now, you can make your own happiness."

They got out of the car and went in the main entrance for Crowne-n-Dale, Inc. To their surprise, everyone was gathered around the receptionist desk.

"I'm sorry we're late. I guess we took longer than I thought." Stephanie said.

"You're not tardy." Heath replied. "It's just now eight o'clock."

"Why are we all gathered here?" Monica asked.

"Elaine refused to miss another steam yoga."

"Hot Yoga." Mimi corrected.

"Whatever," Heath continued. "So, one of us will have to tend the phones and watch the door for a while. I didn't want to have to repeat myself, so we are having the meeting here."

Everyone grabbed a chair, and brought it back to the front. Stephanie sat in the one already there; the one behind the desk.

"We've all worked our asses off for the last three days. Thank you. All of the orders are filled, boxed up, and getting shipped out today. I feel a lot better about starting this legal battle with those sales under our belt. The next few days I have meetings with the lawyers, police investigators, and the private detective. We're still in a hell of a bind, but the strides we made this weekend will help." Heath turned to his left." Mimi, you said you have something going on?"

"I'm glad to hear crunch time is over. I have a meeting today for the library fundraiser. I resold the table Crowne-n-Dale bought, and if I go there in person I can swap out the papers without anyone realizing there had been a change."

"Good thinking. We don't need any more scuttlebutt than we already have." He turned back to the rest of the group. "Figure out a rotation to keep this desk manned at all times. Once that's in place, everyone else get out of here. Take a couple days to rest. Enjoy this lull while we have it. While your out, you might want to think about your future; decide if you might be better off somewhere else."

Heath stood up, and pushed his chair back to his office. Mimi said her goodbyes, and left.

"Why don't you guys take off?" Stephane said. "I can answer the phones."

"What? Why? Don't you want a break?"

"I don't want to go home, and see the house I shared with the man that betrayed me. I don't want to waste the money on a hotel. My brain is too caught up in all this to enjoy anything. I need to research divorces, and I've got a computer right here. So, I might as well be productive while I figure out how to close this chapter of my life. Besides, I did most of the paperwork to file for the patents, I'll need to be here to answer any questions that pop up."

"I don't like the idea of leaving you here."

"And I don't like the idea of you guys having to hang around here after you worked through the weekend. Especially, when there is nothing for you to do here. I'm positive the three of you will find something to do."

"Okay, but don't spend all your time working on the divorce. At least look up a couple cat videos; something that will make you smile."

"Red pandas." When everyone looked at Jason with a confused expression, he added. "Look up red pandas. They are cuter than kittens."

"You guys make me smile, and I will look up the panda bears." Stephanie said.

They all put their chairs away, grabbed their coats, and went out to the parking lot.

"Do they think we're really going to be able to go out and have fun, after all this?"

"You heard Heath, he thinks we need to type up resumes, and start looking for a new job."

"I'm not ready to give up on this one, yet." Clint said.

"What do you have in mind?" Jason asked.

"We've done everything we can to help out here. Why don't we go up and see if there is anything we can do to help my Dad?"

"Sounds great." Monica said.

Two hours later they turned a corner and the lake was in front of them. Clint was driving, Monica was in the front passenger seat, and Jason was sprawled out across the back. They drove into Polson, and then turned right to head up the east side of the lake. Fifteen minutes later they pulled onto a private road and followed it to its end. Tess's car was parked in her spot next to the garage. Clint touched the remote clipped to his visor, and the second garage door rolled up.

"The car and truck are both here, so Andrew must be inside."

"It feels good to be here." Monica got out of the car. "This is the only place that hasn't been effected by everything that's happening."

They stepped into the kitchen. Tess was at the sink, doing dishes. The door on the other side of the room swung open and Andrew stepped through. He was wearing double fronted heavy-duty work pants and a flannel shirt. Both were dirty.

"What are you kids doing here? I thought you in the city, helping out at the office."

"There's nothing left to do there. We filled all the orders."

"You did all of that in a few days?"

"We worked through the weekend," Monica replied. "Everyone was there. Even Elaine helped. Mom and Heath are back there, handling the legal issues."

The older man stepped forward and leaned against the counter top. "I didn't think he would push everyone get done that fast."

Clint walked over and touched his father's shoulder. "It was fine, and Mom kept great food rolling in. It barely felt like work."

Andrew smiled at his son, but it seemed forced. It was as if he didn't think the reassuring statement was comforting, after all.

"Are those burns in your pants?" Clint asked.

"Yes," The father looked down. "I've been welding."

Jason came forward and took a closer look at the other man's garments. "I thought you were tinkering in the shop. You look like you've been building an... I don't know... a bridge."

"Maybe I have."

The three newcomers shared looks of confusion.

"I have some work I need to do today."

"We'll come with you," Monica said.

"No." Andrew exhaled before continuing. "What I'm working on is unlike anything you've ever seen before. I want it to be perfect before I show anyone. I just need another day or two."

"Have you guys had dinner?" Tess said drying her hands.

"We had food before we left Missoula," Jason answered.

Andrew went out the door to the garage.

"That was hours ago, and it's almost lunch time, anyway. Go in and get settled. I'll bring a tray of nachos in to you in a little bit."

CHAPTER SEVEN

The next morning, Andrew put down his comb and just looked at his reflection. He looked tired, but the desperation and fear didn't show. He took that to be a good sign. Maybe he could pull this off. His hands smoothed over the lapel of his suit, which was already laying flat. It was tailor made and concealed the effects aging had taken on his body. The grey hairs at his temples had spread out through more of his hair. He had thought about getting hair dye, but that would do nothing for the lines at the corners of his eyes that were now there even when he wasn't smiling.

He looked fine. Being freshly showered and shaved, he was ready to start his trip. He had crossed the line between checking his appearance and procrastinating. It was time for him to go. He stepped into the bedroom and looked around. There wasn't anything for him to forget, because he didn't need any luggage where he was going.

Downstairs he heard the rattling of dishes. He stopped at the door to the dining room, where the kids were picking at their breakfast. Andrew could remember them all sitting at that table since they were in primary school. This was the first time they silently ate anything.

"Good morning." The Dad tried to sound chipper.

They all looked up and grumbled in return before looking back down at their plates. Their elbows were on the table, holding up rounded shoulders and drooping heads. Clint pushed his eggs around his plate.

"You guys need to go out and do something today. Go out and have fun," Andrew said

"We've been go-go-go since this all started, we haven't have time to think about it. We've been betrayed by someone that I considered a father figure." Jason said.

"I know you worked with him a lot, but he's only one person in your life. I'm not going to let you down." Mr. Bower said.

Monica choked on a sob. "He's taken everything from us. My own father took everything I have and left me destitute."

Clint clasped the hand closest to him, and Jason reached across the table and patted her other one. They had always been a team. It was reassuring to see they still were through this tragedy.

"I'm not going to let that happen." Andrew said, letting his determination ring through his voice. "I'm going on a trip today, and I'm going to fix everything."

"Where are you going?" Clint asked.

"Are you going to chase him down?" Monica inquired.

"Our competition already has all our secrets. Just finding him isn't going to undo all the damage."

"Don't worry about it," The older man interrupted. "I have a plan that's going to make it like none of this ever happened. So, you guys don't need to worry about anything."

"You've been grooming us to take over this company since we were in preschool. We need to help you," his son interjected.

"If there were anything for you to do, I would have asked. I have a plan, and it is something I need to do on my own. I will be back this evening, so plan on having dinner here tonight to celebrate."

None of them looked convinced, but they weren't arguing with him anymore.

"Trust me."

With renewed motivation, he headed out the door. It wasn't just his company at stake. It was those three kids' entire future. He would make everything better, because he was the only one that knew how to.

Turning right on highway 35 would take him towards the city. He knew that's where the kids assumed he went. When traffic cleared, he crossed the main road, and instead went up into the hills. He parked in front of the work shop, but didn't bother going in. After locking the car, he went around the side of the building. With all the trips back and forth he had done the last few days, he had worn a path through the grass. He followed it to the mine entrance.

He was about to make history. It was a shame no one would know about it. He wanted to tell everyone what he was doing, but knew that would just complicate things. This was a trip he needed to do on his own. On the upside, if it didn't work, no one else would be the wiser.

The temperature inside the mine was about the same as it was outside, but it was nice to be out of the wind. He ran his fingers through his hair, getting to all back into place. He looked down at the safety gear he had piled up just inside the entrance, and decided to forgo the helmet. He didn't have to worry about a low ceiling in any of his work areas, and this was the one day he was more worried about what he looked like than being injured in a cave in. He grabbed a flashlight and headed down the sloped tunnel.

Everything was just as he had left it the night before. He feared that he was going to find a dire warning from the future telling him not to go. But there was no future version of himself begging him to stay, not even a note cautioning against it. It might be a sign the time machine doesn't even work, or it could mean that it all turns out just like he hoped it will. He turned on the work light, knowing there was only one way to find out.

Aware he had a few minutes of manual labor first, he took off his jacket and hung it on the light tower. Then he pushed the steel structure to the center of the room. The next thing on his list of things to do was disconnect the batteries from the charger. They were so heavy he had to move them one at a time.

Once they were all in place, he used battery cables to string them together. When that was completed, he confirmed they still held a full charge.

With that done, he went over to the work bench and opened the laptop. He tapped his fingers on the wood surface as he waited for the screen to light up. Once it did, he typed in his password. The computer seemed to be running slow, but he knew that was just because he was anxious. Eventually, he did get the program open and ready to start. Only then did he unplug the computer and carry it over to the time machine. He reached up to put it on the shelf that would be waist high once he was inside the sphere, and then connected it to the control panel.

He thought everything was ready, but took a moment to look around the room to see if there was anything he had forgotten. The only thing left for him to do was put his jacket back on. As he slid it up over his shoulders, he could feel the weight of the flashlight in the pocket. Remembering he had it made him realize he didn't need to leave all the work lights on. He went around the cavern turning them off one by one. When the last light was out, the small beam of light brought him back to the apparatus in the middle of the room.

The computer screen glared brightly compared to the pitch-black surrounding it. Andrew stepped up onto the platform and turned off the flashlight. He no longer needed it.

He looked over the equation on the screen, double checking that he had punched all the right numbers in. The machine would run at sixty percent power for ten and a half minutes. He slid the curser to the start button, but didn't select it. After two deep breaths, he had finally calmed his nerves.

One click, and the magnets started spinning. It was the same sound he become accustom to hearing in the mine, only now it was everywhere around him. He closed his eyes. The electromagnet field being created was outside the visual range, so there was nothing to see. Usually ten minutes flew by before you knew it. Sitting there with nothing to do but count every second as it passed made it feel like eternity.

When the magnets stopped spinning, not only was Andrew in absolute darkness, but it was completely silent as well. It was pitch black in a way only being underground can offer, where you instantly lose all sense of direction.

He felt around and found his flashlight. With one click, he had a beam of light reaching across to the far rock wall. In the darkness, he had imagined the walls just out of his reach. Shining the light around proved the cavern's dimensions hadn't changed with time. The walls were still twenty feet away from him. Outside his sphere there were nothing but rocks. None of his equipment was anywhere to be seen. The lack of tools was his first indication he had successfully traveled through time. How much time? He didn't know.

He wanted to rush outside and confirm his achievement, but there were things that needed to be done first. He looked down at the battery gauge. It read fifty-four percent. He had used more power than he thought it would have. If he had used any more, he would have had to recharge the batteries to get home. He hit the off switch, wanting to save every bit of energy to get him back. Then he shut down the laptop.

Once he felt everything was secure, he stepped down through the steel rings. Now was the time to see if he had really done it. There was debris on the mine floor, so he carefully made his way to the surface. He had never been claustrophobic, but still let out a sigh of relief when the warm sunshine hit his face. The light was blinding at first, but after a few seconds of squinting and blinking, he was able to see his surroundings. The mine was still surrounded by Ponderosa pines, but the brush was much higher than the last time he saw it. There was no longer a path leading out. He didn't want to ruin his suit, so he took his time pushing back branches and stepping over logs down to the road.

It wasn't until he was down at the dirt lane that he became concerned. The shop wasn't there. The metal building had been there for sixteen years. He was only supposed to travel back two. Something had gone seriously wrong. Just when he was about to go back and reverse everything he had just done; he saw a concrete truck turn into the driveway just down the hill. He could see the forms in place for them to pour the foundation. If he remembered correctly, that house had been built in 1998. It was a two-mile walk to the lake house. There he would be about to find out the exact date, and figure out what he would do from there.

As he walked along the orchard, he recognized Tess's car driving out. Quickly, he turned his back to the road, not wanting her to see his face. He hoped that Rick would be the only person he would have to interact with. With a last second glance, he was able to see the profile of the driver and confirm it was his cook. Her hair, just like always, was in a bun on top of her head. Only the hair that had just passed his was a rich brown color, and not the grey he had become accustomed to.

When the house came into view, it was as silent as he had hoped it would be. All the windows were dark, everything was shut up tight, and there weren't any cars in the drive. Andrew went around to the back of the garage, and picked up rocks from the landscaping. The fourth one he grabbed was much lighter than the others. When he turned it over, there was a small door on the bottom. He opened it to reveal a house key inside. He put the fake rock back on the ground, and went around to the side door.

The first thing he needed to do was to find out what day it was. If he was as far back as he thought he was, there would still be newspapers delivered to the house daily. It wasn't laying around anywhere, but Tess would not let that happen. He opened the door to the garage. Just inside was a stack of newspapers, with the sales papers on top. Tess would have been looking at them. He picked those up to find what he was looking for. The front page, with the date across the top; May 8, 1998.

Realizing he had gone back twenty years made his knees almost buckle. Was there any point in being there? They hadn't even merged the companies, yet. That was still a couple months away. But he had already spent an hour just walking to the house. It would be such a waste to just turn around and go back to his own time.

Just building the time machine had kept him so busy, he hadn't figured out exactly what he would do when he got there. He assumed two years would be a large enough span to change things, but how would he create that change? Should he confront Rick? He could say they knew about his plans, and he wasn't going to get away with it. That plan was simple, but he knew he wanted to think about it and hoped he would have time to come up with something better. Being this far back in time, that idea wouldn't even work. You can't say you know he will betray a company, when it doesn't even exist, yet. He thought about just leaving himself a note, but then he might stop the merger from happening. That didn't seem like the right thing to do.

"It's easier to get flies with honey than it is with vinegar," he said to himself.

After successfully travelled back in time, it seemed like such a waste to not try to do something to change the future. He could try telling young Rick that they can get the government contracts. That would get them started on it years before they had. He would have to drive to Bozeman, but there was a brand-new pick-up sitting in the garage.

He needed money. Usually, he just swiped his debit card, but didn't think that would be a good idea. The cards in his pocket were all microchipped. A technology that wasn't even in use in the time he was in. Even the issue dates on the card were far into the future. The cash he had wasn't any use, since it was all dated. His wallet needed to stay in his pocket. He went into his study and opened the wall safe. Just as he knew it would be, there was a stack of cash in the back corner. He didn't think he would need much, but grabbed two hundred, just in case.

Then he filled a small ice chest with cold drinks and snacks. He didn't want to stop any more than he had to. Once his bladder was empty, he was ready to start the road trip.

CHAPTER EIGHT

Andrew turned the pick-up into the parking lot and sighed with relief. He had spent the entire five-hour drive worried that he would be pulled over by a cop. He guessed he could say he lost his wallet. That would be easier than explaining why everything inside was dated two decades in the future. He had stopped at two rest areas, so he could use a restroom with minimal interaction with others.

He had a little mantra going in his head; he could do this, it would all work out, and this was all part of the greater plan. He believed this would bring the balance they all needed. It had been an error on his part to go back so far in time, but the more he thought about it, he realized it might be for the best. He could never be the bad guy that could intimidate someone. It just was not who he was. He didn't know the first thing about scare tactics.

The large metal building was divided into four different businesses, all with identical picture windows next to white doors. The Cannondale Inc. sign hung over one of the center units. It was two minutes to six, and the doors were still unlocked. Andrew stepped into the retail space, but didn't bother looking at any of the items on display. At the back there was a classroom/demonstration area. It was dark. Above that was the office Rick and Heath shared. Rick was the only one up there; talking on the phone. He waved.

Andrew waved back, and headed towards the stairs. With

each riser, he told himself he could do it. This situation was ideal for what he had in mind. The phone conversation wrapped up just as he topped the steps. Rick spun around in the chair to face him.

"I just wanted to have a quick word with you. I've heard rumors about some government contracts. I don't know the details yet, but we need to look into them. I'm sure we can get those contracts, then we will triple our revenue." He rushed through the spiel just as he had practiced it.

"What's going on here?" Rick asked.

"I...uh...just wanted to let you know there are more ways this merger could make us money."

The younger man stared up skeptically. "I just got off the phone with Andrew Bower. He's in Missoula right now. I don't know who you are supposed to be."

"Oh, crap." Bower stepped back until the handrail hit his back. This wasn't something he had prepared for, not something he could have imagined happening. Not knowing what else to do, he turned and fled down the stairs.

"Wait, you look just like him, only older."

Andrew turned the corner at the bottom on the steps, and sprinted towards the door without looking back.

"Are you from the future? Do you know something I don't?"

"Oh, shit. Oh, shit," Andrew mumbled under his breath as he pushed open the door and ran outside. He jumped into the truck and fumbled with the keys trying to get them into the ignition. He sat facing the store and was relieved to see no one else came out before he got vehicle started and pulled away.

After two turns, Andrew was back on Interstate 90 and headed west. He set the cruise control to just under the speed limit and tried to calm down. He should have known Rick would figure it out; he was a smart man. But to walk in the middle of a phone call to his younger self, that was just the worst luck.

The industrial complexes gave way to open fields. He was

able to slow his heart rate and breath. With that, he started to think of things from a new perspective. There was no doubt Rick would take what he said seriously, now that he knew it came from the future. The little bit he had said would most likely start a cascade of changes. He drove the rest of the way back to the lake house excited to see what the results would be.

◆ ◆ ◆

When the magnets stopped spinning, Andrew's flashlight revealed a workbench with scaffolding behind it. He sank back in relief to see the familiar items around him. Did that mean he hadn't changed anything? If things had turned out like he hoped, there would be no need for him to build a time machine. Of course, he still had to have a way to get back to his original time. If the time machine still existed, then it made since for the other stuff be brought down here to make it to still be there, right? The time paradox hurt his head. He decided he needed to get back to the surface to see if he had caused any change.

It was dark when he came out of the mine. The flashlight led him down the path to the shop. His car was parked in front of it. He pulled the door open, thankful things were the same as he had left them. The clock on the dashboard said 10:26 pm. He wondered if the kids were waiting for him.

There were no lights on when he pulled up to the lake house. The was strange, because Tess always left the light over the kitchen sink on if she knew they would be getting in late. He parked in the garage and ran into the house.

"Clint. Monica. Jason."

By the time he got done calling out all the names, he stood in the hallway. No one responded. He bound up the stairs, and then went to the left. After quickly rapping his knuckles on the door he opened it.

"Clint? Monica?"

The room was empty. The bed was neatly made. Nothing was out of place. Andrew turned around and ran to the other wing. This time he didn't bother knocking. Silence and darkness were all that awaited him in Jason's room.

He ran back down the stairs and went into the study, where he had an atomic clock. It read April 7th, 2018. 10:43 pm. It was the same day he had left, but the kids weren't there. It must have worked. He must have changed the past. Otherwise they would still be there, waiting for him.

Even though he had been slogging for fifteen hours, he wasn't tired. There was no way he would be able to sleep until he found out what had happened. He hurried to the garage and jumped back into his car.

By the time he rolled down the hill by Evaro, the lack of sleep caught up with him. He turned on the radio and cracked the window. The cool night air blew against his face. There was a truck stop just ahead where he could stop and get some coffee, but he was only ten minutes away from his destination and didn't want to prolong it.

Turning into his parking lot, he was suddenly wide awake. The sign said Crowne, Inc. The merger never went through. He had succeeded in changing the past, now the only question was what exactly had he done?

The code he put in to disarm the security system was incorrect. Of course, Rick and Heath hadn't been there to help him pick one out. He punched in his son's birthday. The light stayed flashing red. It had to be a date, or he wouldn't remember it. The flashing little light sped up. He tried the date he started the business. The light turned green and he exhaled through pursed lips. He didn't have enough confidence to reset the alarm, but did turn the deadbolt on the door to lock himself in.

His office was his destination, but he stopped at the first door he passed. The name on the plate was not familiar to him. The next name was just as foreign. The door across the hall should have been Jason's office. Instead the placard read Amanda Jefferies. He continued, and finally found a placard with name that was known to him. What should have been Heath's office now belonged to his son. It was a relief to know

Clint still worked with him.

There was only one more door at the end of the hall. His office basically looked the same. He sat down at his desk and booted up his computer. While he waited for it to start, he looked at the papers stacked in front of him. Nothing looked out of the ordinary. It was all the normal paperwork that went along with running the company. Yet, he didn't remember writing any of the memos or placing any of the orders he had invoices for.

He put his elbows on the desk and rested his head in his hands. What was he doing? He took a couple deep breaths, and tried to clear his mind. The first thing he needed to do was find out what had happened when he left the past.

The website for the Bozeman Daily Chronicle had an archive search. He didn't know what he was looking for, so he just put in to start the search on the day he was there and end it two days later. If something significant had happened, that should be enough time to have it covered by the news. He scrolled past a few articles that clearly had nothing to do with him before finally clicking on a link.

Local Businessman Found Dead In Shop

A local shop owner was found dead in his store. The police report it didn't appear to be a robbery. The man was found under the balcony with an obvious neck fracture that he appeared to have sustained in a fall.

Andrew didn't read any further. His eyes were drawn to the bottom of the page where there was a link to a related article. He clicked on it, and had his suspicions confirmed. Rick Lane had died in his store just minutes after he had left.

A sudden stomach cramp force Bower to lean over his trashcan, but since he had forgotten to eat there was nothing in his stomach to puke up. That didn't stop him from dry heaving until he was to exhausted to continue. He laid down next to the receptacle and closed his eyes.

When he opened his eyes again, bright sunlight blinded him. His watch said 7:23 am. He wasn't ready to face his son, or any of the strangers that would soon be coming to work. He dropped a quick note on Clint's desk, and headed back to the lake.

CHAPTER NINE

Monica's body woke up before her brain did. The stretch started in her back, and then went all the way down to her fingers and her toes. The long muscles of her legs and arms extended until she took up the length of the bed. It felt good to wake up before the alarm clock went off, and Monica planned on enjoying it for whatever time she had. She refused to open her eyes and see how long it was before the music would start playing and indicate she needed to get up. She hoped for at least fifteen minutes to snuggle with her fiancé.

"Hmm."

She slid her hand across the sheet. It was weird, the sheets didn't feel like eight hundred thread count Egyptian cotton. They kind of felt like a tee-shirt. There was a fuzzy memory of buying pink sheets at Wal-Mart, but that didn't make sense. She did not shop at lower end chain stores, nor did she have pink bedding. Her entire bedroom was white. Obviously, she wasn't awake yet and some of her dream still clung to her. All of that didn't matter anyway, she was going to cuddle until she had to get out of bed.

Rather than finding the love of her life, she found the edge of the mattress. *Why am I on this side of the bed?* You would think she would remember something as significant as getting into the wrong side, but she had already determined she wasn't really awake. Her right hand went out in search of the man that wasn't where she expected him to be. But instead of finding him, she found the other side of the bed.

Something was seriously wrong. Not only was her boy-friend missing, but the bed was way too small. She slept in a California king, there was no way she should be able to touch both sides at once. Yet, there she lay with fingers curled over each edge of the mattress. She must be traveling and forgot about it. Wasn't it normal to forget where you were when you woke up in a strange bed?

She opened her eyes to have her suspicions confirmed. The ceiling was white and thick with 'popcorn' texture. Hang-ing wooden closet doors were just feet from the end of her bed. This wasn't a luxurious white bedroom with its own private balcony. She felt like the walls were closing in on her, then real-ized it was just a small room. It didn't look like a hotel room. She couldn't even image that Motel 6 would be this cramped and dreary. Had she somehow ended up in the servant's quar-ters?

Beep. Beep. Beep.

Instantly she reacted to stop the grating noise. She turned off the alarm clock and laid back down with a sigh, thankful that dreadful noise had stopped. It had interrupted her. She had to figure out where in the world she was, and why was she alone?

She turned and looked at the alarm clock. She had turned it off, not just hit the snooze. Every alarm clock was different, yet she had gone right to the little button that turned it off, without even looking at it. If it really was her first time with the clock, she shouldn't have been able to do that. She should have had to read what the buttons where to know which one to push.

Slowly, like fog lifting, she could remember the alarm clock on the bedside table of the single bed she grew up sleeping in, on the second floor of the house her mother bought in Great Falls with her father's life insurance. She could recall riding her bike to the elementary school just a couple blocks away. The junior and senior high schools were on the other side of town. It was too far to ride, but since her mother taught at the junior high, she had a ride to and from school every day. By then Paul was riding with them. She had been in second grade when he first picked up her mother for a date. By the next school year, they had married and become the perfect family. Monica had opted to attend the local university and saved money by living at home. It was just in the last year she got her own apartment, to go along with her new position with an accounting firm.

One strange dream, one she didn't even remember having, and her apartment she had worked so hard to get suddenly wasn't up to snuff. It paled in comparison to the mansion she had expected to wake up in. Never, not even in her fantasies, would she be able to afford servant's quarters. That must have been a whopper of dream. What was weird was that she had never had a dream that seemed like reality, and was so vivid it made her own life seem like the figment of her imagination.

She folded back the floral comforter and stood up on the worn Berber carpet. It was*n't* something she wanted to sink her toes down into. With a frown, she headed off towards the bathroom. The doors were right next to each other in a space so small, she couldn't bring herself to call it a hallway.

She turned on the faucet marked hot, and got undressed while she waited for the warm water to make it all the way up to her floor. She noticed the cracks in the tiles as she finally stepped into the spray. Maybe the hot steam would help get rid of the uneasy feeling she couldn't shake. Well, at a bare minimum, it would wash the sleep from her eyes and get her started on a day she wasn't eager to begin.

Clint stepped through his mother's front door and set his briefcase down.

"It's about time you came home," Mimi started ranting before she was in the room. "You can't avoid me forever. We need to talk. I know you think you made a statement, but what you don't realize is the only statement you made is what an asshole you are." She stepped into the entry way. "Oh, it's you. I'm sorry you had to hear all that. I thought you were your father. Is he staying late at work?"

"He wasn't at work."

"What do you mean? Did he leave early? Where did he go?"

"No, Mom. He never came in."

Her look of annoyance became one of concern. "Where is he?"

"He's at the lake house. He's been there all weekend? I'm really worried."

"There's no reason for you to be concerned." She patted her son's arm. "This is just a temper tantrum."

"What? Why would he do that?"

Mimi led him into the living room. When they were both sitting she began. "Your father said we were meddling when we first started talking about you getting married to Amanda. As you know, that was when you both were in Sunday school together. I think she was still in diapers. It began as a joke. At least, I was joking. Over the years, you two took it to heart. Andrew never approved of what we did. He said it wasn't funny. He thought we were pressing you into something you didn't want to do."

"Well, that's silly, Mom. All of my life I've had the best example of what a good marriage is. Dad and you have shown me that a relationship is a partnership, with a foundation of being best friends."

"Aw."

"Amanda has been a constant in my life. She's been a friend since before I knew anyone else. Of course, I want to spend the rest of my life with her and have everything Dad and you did. I'm going to head up to the lake house and check with Dad."

CHAPTER TEN

Monica stood in line at the bank, inside the ropes marking off the place for her to stand. Unlike everyone else, she didn't bother playing with her phone. It seemed like too much effort to get it out. Mostly she just stared at the floor, and tried to avoid eye contact with anyone else. There was a long carpet stretched out between the ropes, so her feet were on a utilitarian maroon rug, instead of the beige tiles that made up most of the floor. The person standing in front of her stepped out of view. She shuffled her feet until she was once again about two feet behind him. She sighed, wondering if she would have enough time to eat when she finally got out of the bank, or where she would go.

When she did look up, there was a television on the counter. She rolled her eyes, sure that she would have to watch commercials while she was stuck there. The fact that there wasn't any sound with it made her take a closer look. It was the security camera feed of everyone standing in line. She expected to be looking back at herself, on screen, then realized the camera wasn't with the monitor. She looked around the room, and when she faced the corner behind the tellers, she was looking right at the camera. Well, that had wasted about ten seconds of her wait. Now what was she going to do?

She stared at the television. She hadn't thought about what clothes she put on that morning, and it surprised her to see she was wearing all black. Her expression was grim, and she had dark circles under her eyes. Even her posture was horrible. She looked like an ad for an anti-depressant... before they took the miracle pills.

It's only been three days since the dreams had started. It should be great to have dreams of a prestigious life, but that wasn't the case. Instead, it made her own existence seem small and alone. Her apartment had one time been her sanctuary, now it just seemed cheap and cramped. Not to mention lonely. Where was this guy she was always looking for in her dream, but never saw?

Monica didn't even like her job. Why had she listened to her family when they said to become an accountant? She had a natural affinity for numbers, so it was a logical choice. Well, her mother had wanted her to become a math teacher, but with both her mother and her step father being junior high school teachers, she thought someone in the family needed to pick a different profession. She had followed everyone else's advice, and went into a career field she found stagnant, boring, and a waste of time.

The aptitude test said she was good with numbers. She didn't need a test to tell her that. Math had been her best subject all through school. What the test didn't tell her was that being an accountant would be tedious and repetitive. At first, she had thought she could get a promotion and find a position she liked better. Now, she realized there wasn't a job with the company that held any interest for her. Not wanting to be in her house either left her no place she could go to get away from the depression. Maybe it was time to go to a shrink and see about getting some of those happy pills?

She pulled her shoulders back and lifted her head up high. It was stupid to let silly dreams affect her like this. There was nothing different from last week to this one. Her apartment was the same. Her life was the same. It was crazy to let dreams affect her this much. She looked around, determined to do something other than stare at the floor.

The people around her weren't moping. On the television

screen she could see that a prime example walked in and got in line behind her. He stood up straight, almost like he was standing at attention. He didn't look depressed at all. He looked healthy and in his prime. He wasn't grinning, but he didn't look sad. Just bored.

He looked familiar. She could picture him smiling. Another image of him laughing came to mind. Neither of them matched what she saw on the screen.

Monica spun around to look at him without the aid of a video camera. There was a shine on his shoes, his slacks were pressed, his dress shirt was tucked in and there was a small belt holding the midline of his pants and top in perfect alignment. His hands were clasped behind his back. Her eyes continued up. He was so tall, she had to pull her shoulders back and tilt her head to look at his face. His chin was cleanly shaved and his grey eyes scanned the room over the top of her head. When she didn't look away, his gaze eventually came down and met hers.

"Why did you cut your hair?" she asked him.

With a bewildered expression he turned around, even Monica could tell he was looking for someone behind him. There wasn't anyone there; he was the back of the line. Finally, he turned back around and met her gaze. "I've had this same hair cut for about a decade. It's a requirement for the military and military school."

She felt flustered. Her eyes dropped to the floor, embarrassed about being so forward. Dumbfounded, she couldn't think of a single thing to say. She clutched to her purse, just because it felt good to have something to hold on to.

"You must have me mixed up with someone else," he added.

"I'm so sorry," Monica said, finally looking back up at him and wishing she could just leave. But she needed to get these deposits into her account, so she gave him a meek smile. "You look like someone I know. I usually never talk to people, and the one time I do, I make a complete ass of myself. I don't know how I had you confused with Jason."

It seemed like once she finally found her voice, she couldn't stop using it. She was so humiliated, and stammering only made it worse. By biting her lower lip, she was finally able to make herself stop talking. She was back to staring at the floor, and it no longer seemed like a bad idea. If she had just stuck with it, she wouldn't have put her foot in her mouth.

"Jason?" He sounded surprised. "That *is* my name. How weird is that? The person you had me mistaken with has the same name as me. What are the chances?"

"Next," one of the tellers called out.

Monica glanced over her shoulder, and was surprised to see that she was now the front of the line. They were calling for her to go up to the window.

"Um, I don't know. I got to go." She was already stepping away from him. "Sorry for the mix up."

Focusing on what she had to do next, she pulled the paperwork out, and plastered a smile on her face as she stepped up to the awaiting teller.

"What can I help you with?" The man behind the counter smiled at her.

"Just a couple of deposits."

The paperwork slid easily across the counter. The teller picked it up, and turned to the computer screen. He typed, not needing to ask any questions. Everything he needed to know was on the forms in his hand. Being idle, left her mind time to wander.

The scene she had just stepped away from replayed in her head. What a strange coincidence that he had the same name as the person she had him confused with. She couldn't pull up the image now, but looking at the monitor she could clearly remember this Jason guy and his hair hanging down past his shoulders. As hard as she tried, she couldn't get the image back.

'Will that be all for you, Ms. Lane?"

"Yes." She had been staring off in the distance, but brought her gaze back to the teller's face. "Have a nice day."

"You, too." Even before the words were out of his mouth,

he looked at the line of awaiting customers, motioning for the next one to come up.

Monica turned the other direction, headed towards the door. If Jason was still the head of the line, she didn't want to know. Then she realized he couldn't be, because he was walking in front of her. It didn't seem possible. She had everything in order; quick and efficient as usual. She should have been able to get out well ahead of him. Instead she was on his heels.

Chivalry wasn't dead. Jason went through the door and stepped to the side, giving her room to walk through while he held it open. He gave her the same smile he had had standing in line. He looked like he didn't have a care in the world.

"Thank you."

"Your welcome, Monica," he responded.

She stopped so abruptly, her shoulders shook with the unexpected impact of a shorten stride. The hair on the back of her neck stood up. Slowly, she pivoted on the balls of her feet until she faced him.

"I never told you my name."

He nodded, the corner of his lips turned down. "I know."

"What is this?"

"I don't know."

"Did you listen to my conversation with the bank teller? Or maybe you looked at my paperwork?"

"I swear I didn't. It just popped into my head."

She stepped the rest of the way through the door, not wanted to block the entrance. He followed, letting it close behind him.

"Listen up Jason, or whatever your name really is. I don't know what kind of scam you're pulling, but I'm not falling for it."

"This isn't a scam. Look." He pulled out his wallet, flipped to where is driver's license was displayed, and showed it to her. "My name really is Jason."

The identification card had his picture, and the name Jason Radcliff on it. It appeared to be real. It's not like he could have had one made to match the name she used while he was standing in line.

"How did you know my name?"

"How did you know my name?" He asked back.

"I didn't. I thought you were someone with long hair."

"Someone named Jason?" He smirked, and then his expression softened. "Wait. There's a Hardee's across the parking lot. Let's grab a bite to eat. I bet we will be able to figure out where we know each other from."

She looked up at him. Really looked at him. His short brown hair spiked up on top. That part obviously wasn't familiar to her, but the rest of him might be. She focused on the shape of his face. His nose wasn't too long, nor was it too short. It wasn't crooked. His lips weren't too big, or too small. None of his features stood out on their own, and combined were fairly attractive. There was no epiphany, no sudden realization of where she knew him from. If there were any more answers to be found, she would probably have to talk to him to find them. She looked at the restaurant. There were already a handful of people eating inside, and with the lunch rush there were bound to be more. It was a place she felt safe going to.

"Sure."

She realized she still had the deposit receipts in her hand, and tucked them into her purse. He stepped off the curb, headed straight across the parking lot to the other building. She fell into stride beside him. They walked over the thin strip of grass that separated the parking areas of the two businesses. It was the first nice day of spring. The sunshine was warm on her shoulders. She was glad she had left her jacket in her car.

"Maybe we went to the same high school?"

"I went to a private school, a long ways away from here."

"Oh."

Being the first one to the door, she opened it for him. He smiled and thanked her and he stepped through. She followed him in and directly into the line. He stopped short of the counter to look over the menu. She already knew what she wanted, and stepped around him. She ordered the chicken sandwich, fries and a soda. She quickly said that was all and handed over the cash, avoiding any complications of him trying to pay for her meal. This was not a date. Even with that thought firmly locked in her head, she still stood next to him, holding her empty cup, until he was done ordering. Their conversation picked back up when they walked over to the soda machine.

"Maybe we had a fling during summer break. I used to spend a lot of time up on the rodeo circuit."

"There are people that really hook up with someone they're only going to know for a short time?" She scowled while putting the lid on her now filled cup.

"Yes. There are."

After stabbing a straw into her cup, she raised her eyebrows at him. "Well, I'm not one of them. Anyways, I spent my summers with my family, here."

He sat down at the closest table. Her number was called, so she headed back to the counter. They passed each other as she went back to the table; his order was ready. She sat down at the table and then popped a fry in her mouth. It was too hot, and she had to suck in cool air around it. As soon as she could finally swallow, she followed it with cold soda. She unwrapped the chicken sandwich, giving the French fries time to cool.

She just got her sandwich unwrapped when he slid unto the bench seat across from her. It was nice to have a moment to figure out what she was going to say next. She glanced up to see him dump his fries out on the tray, and then squeeze out three of the little packets of ketchup into the grease stained cardboard he had just emptied. When that was complete, he unwrapped his burger.

"Maybe we knew each other in a past life?" He asked, and then took a bite.

She pursed her lips as she thought about it. It seemed like a reasonable suggestion. She could picture them in the roaring twenties, her in a dress covered in fringe, topped off with a dapper hat. He would lounge around in a Zoot suit. As easily as the image came to her, she knew it wasn't quite right.

"If it was a past life, would we have had the same names?"

He seemed to think about the question, and then she saw his Adam's apple bob up and down as he swallowed.

"Good point." He popped another French fry in to his mouth. He only chewed it a couple times before swallowing. "This is frustrating. I'm used to being the person with the ideas. All my ideas have already been shot down. Usually, thoughts flow freely for me, and to not have anything, not even an inappropriate, sarcastic response, is unprecedented."

"Well, it's not like I'm coming up with anything."

They both bit into their sandwiches. It was rude to talk with a full mouth, and a great chance to figure out what to say next. He wiped some 'secret sauce' from the corner of his mouth.

"Maybe it's childhood memories from when we were little?" she offered.

"I've never had long hair, so I don't think that could be it."

"Not even when you were a young boy? I can't imagine that way back in the third and fourth grade you were a little soldier."

"No." Jason shook his head. "Back then all I wanted was to be a business executive. I made my father take me to his barber. I looked like I had stepped out of the fifties."

She didn't rush into another guess. Not that she had an another one. She nibbled on her fries and watched the people around them come and go. She actually felt relaxed sitting there with him, even when neither of them spoke.

"Do you have a white bedroom that you share with the love of your life?" She asked.

"Um, nope." He shook his head, looking confused. "No white bedroom and no love of my life. Why?"

She had no idea why she had said that. Someday she was going to have to learn to not say everything that popped into her head. His head was tilted to the side, and he was already smirking, so there was no way she could get out of explaining herself.

"For three days now, I've woken up confused. I expect a big mansion, and have a huge disappointment when I open my eyes to my little apartment." She hadn't plan on opening up to him, but it felt good to let it all out. "There's even some dream guy I keep reaching out for that never actually shows up."

"And you think I'm this guy?" One of his eyebrow went up with the question.

"No, not really. I can't even recollect what my dream guy looks like, but my body remembers him. I know, if I rise up so my heels are barely off the floor I'm at the perfect height to kiss him. You're much taller than that. I would have to rise way up on my tippy toes and you would still have to lean down a little. That's what's so hard to understand. If I'm going to run into someone who's going to 'come out of nowhere', why isn't it this Mr. right?"

She stopped talking and looked up at him. He had a fry up to his mouth, like he had started to eat it, but forgot what he was doing. He just stared at her with a dumbfounded look. *Yikes*! she probably shouldn't have said all that.

"Well, you're very honest and forthright."

She gave him a lopsided smile. "I'm not sure if that's supposed to be a compliment?"

"In a world full of people with their own agendas, you're very refreshing." He laughed. "Even if you did bruise my ego."

She looked down, feeling guilty. After swallowing the lump in her throat, she finally looked him in the eyes. "Sorry, I just don't feel that way about you."

"I never thought you were trying to pick me up. The teller that helped me at the bank, she was interested in me. She laughed at the things I said, smiled when she looked at me, and her gaze would linger over me for a few seconds before she would turn back to her computer screen. With you, it's like I'm invisible."

"I see you, just not romantically. With all the weird shit happening, I can't help but notice you." She replied.

"So, we can rule out soul mates that immediately recognize each other."

She knew he was joking, but still felt culpable. She just sat there staring at him, not sure what to say. He spoke up first.

"I know I have a special place in your heart, even if I'm not at the center of it."

There were goosebumps on her arm. She had the same feeling of familiarity she had at the bank. For a second she could see his face with an even more hubristic smile on it and long hair framing it.

"You say that like you're repeating something I've told you a thousand times."

"Maybe you have?" He suddenly didn't seem so sure of himself, like maybe he had picked up on the same eerie sensation she had.

"Or maybe I've never said it."

"Or that."

They both laughed, even though nothing seemed funny anymore. He finished up the last bite of his burger, and she polished off her fries. They avoided eye contact, and didn't know what to say. Things seemed even stranger than they had at the bank.

CHAPTER ELEVEN

Monica's smile faded as soon as she opened her eyes. The first thing she saw was the bedroom window, and it looked tiny. It hadn't seemed small when she rented the place, but when you wake up expecting a big picture window looking out at lovely scenery, something only two feet wide pales in comparison. To be honest, she hadn't even considered it before. She used to think a bedroom window as just something you had to put thick curtains over to keep the room dark during daylight hours. Other than in these elaborate dreams she kept having, she never had a beautiful view to look out on when she woke up.

Sitting up in bed, she realized she didn't feel as bad as she had the day before. The memories of Jason clung to her, surrounding her with his aura of confidence. At a minimum, she wasn't alone. There was someone else that seemed to have some weird connection to her.

She got out of bed and grabbed her cell phone. There he was listed in her contacts. *He has to be real if he's in my phone, right?* Just the thought that he might not be real made her question how tenuous her grasp on reality really was. Could the sudden depression be a sign of an even bigger mental disorder? Could she have imagined the entire thing? She could clearly remember getting his phone number just before they left the fast food place, and she put it directly into her phone so she wouldn't lose it.

The fact that he was listed there meant he was real, right? The only other option was that she added the new contact in her sleep. She had never walked in her sleep, so adding a new phone number into her cell phone seemed unlikely. Could she have imagined the whole thing? Damn it, she couldn't be a hundred percent sure that she hadn't. She pulled up the text message screen and typed 'Are you real'?

She hit send, and then immediately wanted to undo it. It was one thing to act a little crazy when you were home alone, it was another thing entirely to send out messages announcing it to others. She held the phone up to her lips, while she prayed for a return message saying there was an error and it could not be sent.

"Please. Please. Please."

The pleading didn't help. Her phone didn't chime. She even checked to make sure it wasn't on silent. The volume was turned up. There were no incoming messages. Disgusted with herself, she put down the phone and went to the bathroom. It was probably a wrong number anyway. Even if she had met him, he probably wouldn't have told her the right one. Who would give their right information to some nut case talking about dreams that make her downcast even though she has a perfectly good life?

She was on the toilet peeing when the phone chimed. She tried to stop midstream and stand up, but just ended up trickling urine down her legs. She sat back down, and wiped her leg with a wad of tissue. Trying to stop midstream made her urethra spasm, and it took forever for it to relax and let her bladder fully drain. She tapped her feet until she could finally jump up, pull up her pajama bottoms and run into the other room. The incoming message said 'Yes, I'm real. It's reassuring to know you are too. How about dinner tonight?'

That was a relief. Not only was he polite enough to not point out how strange she was, he wanted to get together again. But was seeing him two days in a row really a good idea? Holding the phone in her lap, she looked around. The pictures on her wall were all framed posters she had picked up at flea markets and yard sales. What had seemed eclectic when she put them up, now looked shabby. But it wasn't as depressing as it had been the day before. There was something else occupying her thoughts, other than all the things she didn't have. It was like a ray of sunshine coming through the parted drapes.

◆ ◆ ◆

Monica was late as she drove past the restaurant. Cursing under her breath, she turned on her turn signal and pulled into the parking area. She was usually very punctual, and it frustrated her that a lot of little things from leaving work late to a traffic accident all conspired to keep her from being on time.

After getting out of the car, she pressed the button to lock it. The horn chirped, indicating she had. She was in the middle of the block, looking directly across the street at where she needed to go. The responsible thing to do would be to walk down to one of the intersections and use the cross walk, but as she walked up there was a lull in the one-way traffic. So, she stepped down off the curb and jogged across the three lanes before the cars two blocks away caught up with her. She then walked into the door under the sign 'Celtic Cowboy'.

The podium just inside the door had the sign turned to 'Please Wait To Be Seated', but she could see Jason just two tables away. The hostess was headed her way, so Monica waved her off and motioned to Jason. The young lady nodded that she understood, and went back to folding napkins at the bar. After putting a smile of her face, she turned to the man waiting for her. He leaned back in his chair, looking like he had been there for a while. There were two glasses of wine on the table. He picked up the glass closest to him, and took a sip, never taking his eyes off her.

"Who's that for?" Monica pointed at the glass closest to her.

"You," Jason said with a smile and put his glass down.

His arrogance oozed off him. This wasn't the type of person she normally hung out with, and definitely not someone she would date. She rolled her eyes, not concerned in the slightest he was staring right at her as she did it. His shit eating grin never changed. With a sigh, she sat down across from him.

"I never drink wine."

"So, you've never tried it?"

She shook her head. He let go of his glass and folded his hands in his lap. "Think of it as a test. When I came in here, I thought 'what would Monica like to drink?' and Merlot jumped into my head. If your name jumped into my head, why can't other things about you?"

Her fingers tapped on the table. So, it was an experiment. One sip wouldn't hurt. She picked the glass up and swirled the contents. Leaning down, she drew in the fragrance. It was an earthy smell, with a whiff of oak, current and a little bit of caramel. So far so good. The aroma held appeal. When she looked up, Jason was watching her. *Does he think I'm a freak?* Why was she sniffing the wine? Had she seen it in a movie? With a sigh, she realized she was overthinking it. It was just a way for them to investigate, and all she had to do was taste it. The rich flavor enveloped her tongue. She took a moment to savor the complexity. Then, she finally swallowed. When she looked up he was quiet, but had one eye brow raised.

"Okay. It's good," she admitted.

He leaned back with a smug smile. "I told you, I know you better than you know yourself."

She choked, and was glad she hadn't taken another sip. He really was cocky. Folding her hands in her lap, she never broke eye contact with him.

"Well, if you know me so well, then order my dinner."

"All right."

He picked up the menu and studied it. At first, she thought he was just being dramatic, and then she realized he was reading every line item. She had assumed he would look at it from a new perspective, to guess what she wanted. But he looked like he was reading it for the first time.

"Haven't you been here before?"

"Nope," he said without looking up. "I'm new in town. Just transferred to the Air Force base last week."

That didn't feel right to her. She was sure she knew him, and assumed he had attended the local schools. She had imagined they had been in the same elementary school. A childhood connection would help explain the feeling of familiarity she had with him. The idea of him being just another blue uniform that came in and out of town didn't match up with anything she thought she knew about him. The waiter coming to the table distracted her from her thoughts.

"The lady will have the Sheppard's pie with a side salad, and I will have the corned beef and cabbage with French fries."

"And what kind of dressing with the salad?" The server looked at her, but she didn't answer. She locked eyes with Jason and waited for him to respond. The corners of her mouth threatened to turn up.

"Italian."

"Anything else?"

"No," Jason said. "That will be all."

The waiter when back towards the kitchen, leaving them staring at each other. "Well, that's not exactly..."

He raised a hand between them, stopping her from finishing the sentence. "I figured what you really wanted was the Irish Cobb salad, and I would have ordered that for you if that was white wine." He motioned towards the glass in her hand. "But merlot goes much better with red meat."

"That's unnerving."

The silence was thick in the air. The clanging of silverware on plates and chatter from nearby tables didn't seem to reach them. She unfolded the napkin and set it in her lap. It was a nervous reaction. All the ease she had had being around him dissipated. Jason cleared his throat, and the sound brought her eyes up to him. He gave her with a lopsided smile. It reassured her, even if it was goofy.

"I was thinking that maybe this is like a Jungian psychology thing, and we've just tapped into the collective unconscious." Jason said.

Her headed tilted side to side as she tossed the idea around. She looked over his head, not actually seeing anything in the room. When her eyes finally met his, she could feel her brows pulled down with deep lines between them.

"If that were the case, wouldn't we know things about everybody? Have you had this happen with other people?"

His eyes dropped to the table and he shook his head. "No, just you."

He reached down on the floor, and grabbed a knap sack she hadn't noticed. Suddenly he had her attention, so she sat up a little straighter. He pulled out a sketch pad and slid over to the seat next to her. He flipped through the pages like he was looking for something specific. She stole glimpses of sketches as he flipped through. From what she could see, he was a good artist. He finally found what he was looking for and showed her a depiction of a large house. It was very detailed.

She gasped and her hand went to her chest. After a couple deep breathes, her hand tentatively touched the page, as if she would be able to reach through it to the place it represented.

"That's it. That's the house in my dreams. How…" She looked up into his grey eyes, unable to ask the question. It's wasn't just being unable to find the right words, she didn't know what she even wanted to ask.

"I don't know," he answered without any trace of the smirk that usually adorned his face. "I've drawn as long as I can remember, but suddenly in the last week, I'm sketching things I've never laid eyes on before."

He turned the page and it was another view of the same house. In this one, you could see the lake behind it. There were three gables along the roof, all with large picture windows underneath them. The ground floor had even more glass. Shrubbery littered the ground below the windows.

"That balcony there leads to my bedroom." She pointed

to the exact one she meant.

Once again, the silence stretched out between them. Being around him felt like a roller coaster ride. One minute they had a camaraderie of lifelong friends, and then the next it was so eerie goosebumps covered her arms.

He looked at her, and then back down at the paper.

"Would that make you my sister?"

"What?" she asked.

"I think I lived in this house," he said. "Why else would I be drawing it? You think you lived there, too. I must admit, I've never felt like this with any other woman. I really like spending time with you, even though I don't want to get into your pants. We don't look alike, but why else would two people live together if they weren't family?"

"I don't know, but I know what you mean. Brotherly love is the best way to describe what I feel towards you."

"I feel like they were trying to figure out something there isn't be an answer to. Admittedly, I have very little experience with strange or mystical things. Being Air Force Intelligence, my world was all about finding evidence and seeing where it leads. All we have is hearsay, at best, and it all points away from anything rational."

He turned the page. Instead of another view, it was a portrait.

Monica gasped. The hand that rose to cover her mouth shook. Suddenly she was at the University of Montana, walking out of the library with the man of her dreams... her life long friend. She noticed another student walk into the building looking at him. She wasn't the only one to notice how attractive he was. He spent most of his evenings with her, a dumb kid just starting her freshman year, when he could be dating anyone he wanted to.

"I really appreciate everything you've done to help me settle in here, but isn't there someone else you'd rather spent your time with?" She asked in the memory.

"What?" He turned to her. The charcoal drawing Jason had

done didn't show his eye color, but reminiscing they were dark chocolate brown with gold specks in them.

"Don't you have a girlfriend?" She had been so nervous, she had barely got the question out.

"No." He smiled.

"Well, there's got to be someone else you'd rather spend your time with. I see other women check you out all the time." She motioned to the door that closed behind them.

His eyes flickered over her shoulder. She could tell by the way he pursed his lips he knew exactly what she was talking about. His eyes came back to her face and studied it.

"I haven't noticed anyone I would rather be with. How about you? Do you have someone else you'd prefer to spend your evenings with?"

"No." Her eyes shot to the ground, and her cheeks became hot.

"Good. Then I won't feel bad about monopolizing all of your time."

When she looked back up he kissed her. Right then she knew that fairy tales did come true. Or at least they had. Then the memory dissipated as easy as the relationship had.

"You know who this is?" Jason asked

She pried her eyes off the piece of paper and looked up at the artist. "That's the man that never appears in my dreams. The man that I'm going marry. How can I pretend he's a figment of my imagination when I'm looking at a picture of him?"

"So, you recognize him?"

"Yes."

"The same way you recognize me?"

She had to think about it, but finally answered, "Yes. I don't know how I met him. I can't even imagine him in this town, but I know him the same way I know the layout of that house."

He put the sketch pad away, and went back to the seat across from her. When she exhaled, her whole body shook. She closed her eyes and took deep breaths until she was sure she wouldn't cry. When she did finally look up, he sipped his wine and gave her a reassuring smile. To her surprise, she could smile back.

Their food was delivered. They kept the conversation generic, avoiding any topics that might trigger more emotions. Mainly she told him about Great Falls, what places he should visit and what businesses to avoid.

"So, want to get together tomorrow night?" Jason asked, pushing his empty plate away from him.

"I would love to, but I can't. I've got something else I have to do."

CHAPTER TWELVE

Monica stood on the second-floor balcony, with the biting wind at her back. Her fingers tapped at her sides, waiting for her knock to be answered. She hoped she had the right place. Jason opened the door and frowned at Monica. He leaned against the frame, blocking her from going into his apartment. "I thought you had more important things than hanging out with me tonight?"

"I did," she retorted, motioning to the dress she was wearing. "I've been at my Grandparent's fiftieth anniversary party."

He backed away from the entrance, opening the door further. The corner of his mouth slightly curled. "I suppose that's a good enough reason to ditch me for the night." He looked down at his watch, as she walked over the threshold. "I guess after being married for fifty years, I'd be headed to bed at eight o'clock, too."

"Oh, the party was still going. They were playing couple's games when I left."

There were no frills in his apartment. The living room held a chair, sofa, coffee table and a television that was tuned to a basketball game. There wasn't anything along the lines of decorations or personal touches. There were a couple of unpacked boxes tucked away in the corner that might hold that stuff, but she doubted it. The recliner was pointed at the TV, and the table next to it had all the remotes and a can of beer, so she assumed that was his spot. She sat down on the couch.

"I'm sorry if the couples' games depressed you." He said sitting down in the chair. "I've never been in love, so I don't what it's like to miss someone when they're no longer there."

His concern was touching. He was the only person, other than her mother, that would jump to the conclusion that she needed comforting. It felt good to have someone there for her, even if his worry was misplaced.

"Um, thank you, but that's not why I'm here." She dug through her purse and finally found the sheets of paper she was looking for. "They were playing this game where a couple that's newly wed, one that's been married twenty years and one that's been married fifty years all answer questions about their spouse while in separate rooms, and then they are brought together and see which couple knows each other the best."

She started to hand him the list, but stopped. "So, I was thinking we could do this not only as a test of each other, but as a test about ourselves. When you read the question, first answer about yourself. Not what you know, but whatever pops into your head right after you read it. I think we need to tap into our subconscious for this to work. If we do, we might be able to learn more about these memories that keep surfacing. So, just answer with the first thing that comes to mind. Then answer the question again for what you think my answer is. When we're done, we can compare."

With a nod he stood up and went over to the mystery boxes in the corner. After digging around for a few minutes, he turned around with two pens and binders. "So we have a hard surface to write on," he explained.

On the drive over, she imagined having to do a lot more convincing, or at least explaining, to get him to go along with it. To her surprise, he seemed to grasp the idea immediately and willingly joined her. Soon, the only sound in the room was the scratching of pen tips on paper as they jotted down their answers. She looked over at Jason, to see him lost in thought staring off into the corner. She quickly looked down, not wanting to get caught peeking at him instead of writing down her own answers.

"They had your grandparents answering these questions about their sex lives?" Jason asked.

At first, she didn't know what he was talking about, then she looked a little further down the list. She dropped her pen as her hand came up to cover her gaping mouth.

"Oh, I hadn't noticed those." She cringed. "It's a game so I assume they wanted everyone to play, but I have to admit I'm glad I left before I heard those answers."

"So, are we going to go there... Oh wait. I know the answer to that one." He smiled and his left eyebrow went up and down before he scribbled down what he had thought of.

How would he know the answer to any intimate questions about me? It was obvious we've only been platonic friends, wasn't it? She studied him, wondering if she knew what he looked like naked, and just hadn't recovered the memory. Finally, she shook her head sure that couldn't be the case. She was way too comfortable with him for there to ever have been anything sexual between them. Reassured she didn't need to worry about what he was writing; she went back to her own list.

By the time she put her pen and paper down, he was already done and sitting crooked in the chair to face her with a mischievous grin. She feared it was going to be a complete waste of time, but he seemed to be having fun at least.

"Okay, first question." She read from the paper. "What is my favorite musical group?"

"I have to admit; I didn't like this question." Jason's smile wilted. "I couldn't think of a band for you. I couldn't get that specific. I just put eighties music."

She laughed, and showed him where she had written 'anything eighties' on her own sheet. Not only did they match on that answer, she was right with her guess that he liked AC/DC. She'd figured their answers would be similar, but she hadn't expected them to match word for word. She thought the game would be fun, but the reality was turning out to be a little uncanny.

"Okay, with the next question, I've never been sailing, but it popped into my head as soon as I read the question. I feel like I've been out boating with you," she said,

"Probably have been, since I put sailing for both my answer and yours."

When she looked up, his smile was gone. He didn't even have the mischievous grin he'd had while writing down the answers. The light joking feeling was gone. A somber silence settled over them, as neither of them were in a rush to get to the next question. He drank from his beer can, tipping it high as he drained the last of the contents. "Want one?" He held up the empty can. She said yes, so he went to into the small adjacent kitchen to get them.

"Maybe 'they' deleted our memories?" She asked.

"You mean like the government?" He gave her a skeptical look over the refrigerator door.

She couldn't believe she was about to say this. Was it possible they were reduced to conspiracy theories? "Well, 'they' usually is some type of government agency."

"What would they have to gain from doing that?" He asked.

"Apparently, a lot of money," she responded. "I was pretty rich in this other life. I mean I had servants. That money had to go somewhere."

"So, you're assuming the other life is the real one, and the one you're in is the made up one. It would be simple to mess with someone's memories, but changing their whole life would be monumental. I think other people, like your parents, would suddenly noticed if you moved to a new house, new city, and just happened to suddenly lose a couple million dollars."

They both sat silently sipping their beers. What he said made sense. The number of people affected by the changes from one life to another would be astronomical. Someone else would have spoken up. Another theory shot down.

"I think we're on the right track to figuring this out. Let's continue with what we were doing." Jason said.

She nodded, letting go of her frustration. He was right that they needed to press on.

"Alright, what kind of present would I like best?" He asked.

"Travel?" she asked with a shrug. She could see herself dropping him off and picking him up from the airport.

"Yep, and for you I put diamonds. That just might be because I know you're longing for your engagement ring."

She rolled her eyes. "Diamonds are in a lot more than just wedding sets. There are earrings, necklaces, tennis bracelets and pennants. They are my birthstone."

"So, I got that one right?" He took a long sip from his beer can.

"Yes. So, what is my favorite way to spend an evening?" She turned in the seat to be able to see him over the top of the paper.

"I can picture you being very boring and spending every night working. Of course, you have a glass of wine while you do it." The disapproval was very clear in his voice, at the working long hours not the consuming alcohol part.

"If I had a job that I liked, I could see myself being very content doing that. As long as I was challenged. Nothing about my current work inspires me to do it a minute longer than I have to." She looked down at her paper. "I image you spend most your nights out picking up chicks."

"Is there a better way to pass a night?"

Monica laughed and shook her head at his comment and then read the next question. "Okay, good. We're getting back to more serious questions. What is my favorite way to be soothed?"

He gave a little smirk and leaned back in his chair. "You want to talk about it."

"While you just want to eat. Macaroni and cheese. Mashed potatoes. All the comfort foods to console you."

They didn't have to confirm that the answers were correct anymore. They weren't even shocked that they were getting them all right. It was just confirmation of what they already believed; they knew each other a whole lot better than two people who'd only know each other a few days. It was like they had spent a lifetime together, but where was this life... or when?

"The question we all've been waiting for," he said. "What turns me on sexually?"

"Anything female?" she sassed back.

"Oh, how right you are," He leaned back in his seat and folded his hands in his lap. "Unfortunately, you're not as easy as I am, but I think I know... a deep voice is what cranks your shaft."

A shiver ran down her spine as she thought about Sam Elliot's voice. This time Jason did want confirmation that he had given the right answer, but the heat climbing her face seemed to be all the response he needed.

The questions continued, and they finished off a couple beers. The silly game was more fun than she'd had in longer than she remembered. She hadn't had a night like this since her best friend had gone off to college, and never came back. She didn't realize how lonely she had been until she had something to compare it too. Maybe the depression had more to do than just wanting a fancy house. She already could feel her soul healing front the light banter that passed between them.

"Maybe we ought to try getting hypnotized?" Jason asked.

CHAPTER THIRTEEN

The address was for a small building that obviously started out as someone's home before being turned into an office when the neighborhood was swallowed up by the business district. The placard on the door listed three companies. The small foyer had doors immediately to the left and the right, but the one they were looking for was at the back of the building across from the door labelled restroom.

A man met them at the entrance and ushered them into the room. He was only a few inches taller than Monica, but his fuzzy hair added a couple inches to that. Looking around the room, it looked like a study with bookshelves along two walls, dark leather furniture, and lamps in each corner lit the room without the glare of fluorescent lights.

"I'm Owen. What can I help you with, today?"

Sinking into the cushy chairs, she glanced over at Jason. He was so confident and laid back... completely opposite of how she felt. She picked at the thick seam of the arm rest and wished she could emulate him. On the drive there, he said he was sure this would give them answers. To her, it all sounded too good to be true.

"I'm Jason and this is Monica. We want to be hypnotized."

The comment was dismissed with a wave of his hand. "I figured that much. What I need to know is what you want to achieve from our session? I assume by looking at both of you that you're not looking to lose weight." He laughed at his own joke. "Do you want to quit smoking, stop gambling, or just give yourself a stronger self-image? What is the message you want implanted in your thoughts?"

In a sudden panic Monica turned to Jason. He crossed his legs, leaning back in the chair. She was on the edge of her seat with her nails digging into the arms. How could he be relaxed after hearing a comment like that? She glowered at him, and he didn't seem to notice. She turned back to the man across from them. "We don't want anything 'implanted', we just want to re-cover lost memories."

The hypnotist looked at Jason, as if seeking confirmation. She was instantly irritated at needing to have a man verify what she said. Thankfully, Jason was smart enough not to reply. It might have something to do with the dirty look she gave him.

"Well, that's not really what I do. I give you positive thoughts that help mold you into the person you want to be." Owen said with a serene expression.

This is what she had been worried about. Her brain was something she didn't want messed with. The man sitting across from her had a paisley tie and lilac shirt that were a shade or two off from actually matching, didn't seem to understand that. His reassuring smile was anything but, and he seemed completely oblivious to her panic.

"This isn't going to work," Monica said to Jason. "I don't want anything else put into my brain." He didn't respond to her. He just put his hand on hers and directed his comment to the other man.

"Do you know of anyone that specializes in recovering blocked memories?"

"No, I don't" Owen leaned back in his chair. "I've heard of some psychotherapists trying it a long time ago, but they were never able to determine if the memories were really recovered or if they were implanted during the process. The going therapy for people that believe they've recovered memories they'd pre-viously blocked out is to treat the trauma they associate with those memories. Unfortunately, I don't even know who to refer you to, since this is so far out of my realm. Though, I have to say, the thought of being able to access a part of one's life that was previously unreachable is fascinating."

No one spoke. Well, at least this craziness was over before it even began. All of her angst had been for nothing. Her mind was safe because the man with the gap between his front teeth wasn't going to mess with it. Monica gathered her purse, assuming they would be leaving soon. To her surprise, Jason seemed to have other ideas.

"Would you be willing to put me under and ask me a list of generic questions? Then asked them all again after I'm fully conscious. I'm just curious if there would be any variations in the answers."

Owen clasped his hands together and rested his jaw on top of them while he thought about it. "If I stuck with open ended questions that gave no hint at the answer I was expecting from you, this just might work. Of course, without any prompting, the both answers will most likely be the same."

Jason shrugged.

"Let me compile a list of things to ask you." He went over to the desk in the corner and rummaged through the drawers.

What just happened? They were all but headed out the door. The hypno-therapist said he couldn't do it, there was no reason to waste any more of his time. Now, she was really alarmed. Monica turned towards Jason, taking both his hands in hers. "I don't think this is a good idea."

"I know. That's why I didn't ask you to do it."

She rolled her eyes, wishing she could shake some sense into him. He obviously missed her point. If she didn't think it was a good idea for her to do it, she didn't think he should do it, either. How could he not understand that?

"All of this is so bizarre. What if someone is trying to brainwash us? They could already be implanting thoughts into our heads. Trying to access those might trigger an unforeseen reaction. I don't want to do something that could end up changing who you are as a person."

"Like, I could wake up and suddenly think kale taste good?" He feigned concern.

Her breath came out in a puff. If he wasn't going to take any of this seriously, how was she supposed to get through to him? Maybe if she smacked him upside the head, she might get her point across. She held tight to the arm rest to keep from actually doing it.

"You're right. We might be some experiment into the power of positive thinking. Make us dream about a great life, and see if we make that life come true. I think the worst that might happen is that I'd remember having the false memories implanted. If not, that's what I have you here for," Jason explained. "I trust you. If it doesn't seem right, stop it. Even if you can't, you can tell me what happened so I'll know what's real and what isn't."

She realized he wasn't willing to risk everything. He trusted her to be in control when he couldn't. He wasn't blowing her off, he was relying on her. Even though they had only known each other less than a week, he still had faith in her. She had assumed he rushed into this without thinking things through. Ends up he had thought about it, and came to the conclusion he could rely on her to get him through it.

He was right. She would.

Owen sat back down in front of them with a new gleam in his eyes. "You know this is just a test of an abstract theory. I'm not going to prep you before the questions, like having you go to a specific place or time. I expect the answers to be the same because of that, but because this is a test, and only a test, I want to keep everything generic as possible. Are you ready?"

Before answering, Jason looked at her. It was touching that he made sure she was on board, first. Since it was generic questions, and she would be there to yell stop if anything seemed wrong, she gave him a nod.

Owen took a bronze medallion on the end of a long chain out of the table drawer next to him and swayed it gently. Jason's eyes locked onto it. Monica intentionally looked away from it and tuned out the soothing sound of Owen's voice. She was too tense to fall under its effects, but didn't want to take a chance. She let out a pent-up breath when he finally started asking questions.

"What is your name?" The hypnotist leaned back against the dark leather chair and folded his hands across his stomach; the gold medallion discarded on the side table.

"Jason Ethan Radcliff."

Monica scanned her friend from head to toe, looking for any signs of distress. To her relief, he was very relaxed. Slumped against the back of the chair, his face was completely slack, giving her no indication of how he was doing. But there wasn't anything to give her concerns, so far.

"How old are you?"

"Twenty-three."

Her eyes went back and forth between the two of them as they spoke. Neither of them moved, and their tone was very monotonous. It was all very boring.

"Where do you work?"

"I work at my father's company. I'm in research and development. I'm the one that turns the ideas into products we can sell."

What? Where did that answer come from? Holy shit, it was working. She sat up, paying close attention to what he said.

"Where do you live?"

"I travel a lot, so I don't really have a place I live at. I even get my mail at my office and have it forwarded to wherever I'm at, at the time. But, if you ask where my home is, I would have to say Flathead Lake. That's where I'm at when I'm not on the road."

No wonder he drew pictures of it, it sounded like the only place he considered home. Was she like him? Did she travel a lot, only stopping at the lake house when she was in town? No, that didn't seem right for her. She didn't think the jet set life would suit her in either life.

"Are you married?"

"No."

"In a relationship?"

"Only with myself. I'm the only one with me everywhere I go."

She expected him to laugh after that comment. She could hear it in her head, even if it didn't actually happen. It made her feel like it was just a shell of him, a hollow person without emotions answering the questions. This was what she'd feared, but she couldn't bring herself to say 'stop'. She was too interested in what he was going to say next.

"How do you know Monica?"

"We grew up together. Our fathers are business partners."

"All right, that's all the questions I have for you. At the count of three you are going to wake up and not remember anything we've talked about. One. Two. Three." Owen snapped his fingers.

Instantly, Jason came back to himself. His back was once again perfectly straight. She could see the corner of his mouth move as he chewed on the inside of his lip, and his eyes questioned everything as he looked back as forth between Monica and the man across from them. "So, when are we going to get started?"

"Right now," Owen said with a smile. "What is your name?"

"Jason Ethan Radcliff." His voice was relaxed, like the first time he answered the question, only this time there was a little, very slight, emotion laced with it.

"How old are you?"

"Twenty-three."

"Where do you work?" Owens voice grew monotonous asking the same questions over again.

"I'm in the Air force."

Owen's body jerked and his eyes shot to Monica. She just nodded. It was like he didn't believe what he heard until he got confirmation. She flicked her chin, motioning for him to continue. Jason noticed the little go between, but didn't say anything.

"Where do you live?" The businessman was on the edge of his seat, no longer able to keep his voice level.

"Here. In town. I just got an apartment."

"Are you married?"

"No." Jason's curiosity over Owen's reaction seem to fade as he answered one boring question after another.

"In a relationship?"

"No."

Was there a little longing in his voice? That one-word answer wasn't anything like the flippant response he'd given before. She filed that thought away, not wanting to be distracted from what was being asked next.

"How do you know Monica?"

Unlike before, Jason flashed her a quick smile before answering, "I just met her at the bank. I've only known her for a few days."

"That's the last of the questions," Owen leaned back in his chair.

Everyone was silent. Owen looked like he was trying to figure out what had happened. Monica was too, but she'd already ruled out all the ideas that were flashing through his mind. She looked over at Jason, who looked like he was patiently waiting.

"Is this the part where you hypnotize me and ask them all again," Jason inquired.

"We already did that," Monica said and squeezed his hand. "And..."

"It's amazing." Owen looked like he was no longer sorting theories in his head. "Some of the questions were exactly the same, like name, age, and relationship status. The other ones were like talking to two different people. It's unbelievable. You guys have known each other in two different life times."

Monica filled Jason in on the answers he didn't remember saying and didn't bother sharing their theory they wouldn't have had the same names in a past life. She finishing up with, "I need to make a phone call."

He didn't say anything, just handed her the keys to his car. "What's this for?"

"So, you can sit down and be comfortable while you talk," he responded. "And you can lock the doors, so I don't have to worry about you standing on the street corner while distracted by your conversation. Then, I can take my time in here, since I won't have to protect you, and I can give you some privacy."

She scowled at him, but took the keys and walked out of the office. The car was warm inside with the spring sunshine coming in the windows. She sank down in the plush leather seat. She even reached up and hit the lock button on the arm rest, even though the felt silly doing it. After dropping the keys in the cup holder, she pulled out her cell phone and dialed her mother.

"Hey, honey. What is going on?"

It was good to hear her mom's voice. It was always comforting, and nice to know she had someone that would be there, no matter what.

"Hey Mom, what are you doing?"

She wasn't avoiding the subject. Really, she wasn't. This wasn't something she wanted to drop on her mom if she was in the middle of something. She didn't want her mother to be distracted during this conversation.

"I was just pulling up weeds in the flower beds. What's up?"

Good, she is alone. Monica didn't have to feel guilty about bringing up something personal while her mother was with other people.

"I want to talk about my biological father."

This was so awkward. She had avoided the subject her whole life, because she didn't want her mother to feel bad about being a single parent. Her father was dead, so it wasn't like she could look him up and get to know him. Then she had a new Dad, one that really cared for her. After that, she didn't want to bring up her dead father, for fear her step-father would think she didn't really love or appreciate him. His feelings were more important that any curiosity she might have had.

"Oh, okay." The older woman sounded a little surprise. "Give me a second to brush some of this dirt off me and sit down on the porch."

She could hear rustling around on the other end of the line, and a clunk, like a spade being put down. Then it was quiet. She imagined her mother taking a deep breath and preparing herself for the conversation.

"What do you want to know?"

"I really know nothing about him. I've never asked before. What did he do for a living?" She heard her mother sigh, and assumed it was in relief.

"He was the CEO of a company."

"What kind of company?" Monica asked.

"They specialized in equipment used by police officers."

Monica had hoped that starting the conversation would start her mother reminiscing. Instead, she was having to pull the information from her one answer at a time. It made her feel like her mother was hiding something.

"He made a lot of money." Her mother filled the silence.

"What?"

"I assume you are asking about this because you've found out what I'm really worth."

"Um, no," *What was going on?* She'd known her mother would be uncomfortable talking about her first husband, but it was becoming apparent she didn't understand why. "What are you talking about?"

"Your father was a very rich man. When he died, he owned fifty percent of the shares of Cannondale Inc. I had no interest in filling his shoes, so I let his business partner buy out the half I suddenly owned."

"I know about that. You used the money to buy the house."

Her mother laughed. "Buying the house barely took half of it."

"Tell me you don't have hundreds of thousands of dollars

sitting in a savings account."

"Of course not, dear," the older woman said. "There really isn't that much left. Your college took a large chunk out of it. I've had to dip into for other things, like a new roof and a furnace. I feel so guilty every time I must; I know that money is for you. You will inherit it when I pass."

"You feel guilty for spending my father's money to keep me in a warm, dry home? Mom, that doesn't make sense. He was your husband more than he was my father, so the money belongs to you just as much as it does to me. And since I never really knew him, I would rather that you use it to retire comfortably than horde it away for me."

"It warms my heart to hear what an incredible person you've turn into."

She rolled her eyes. "Well, that's your fault, Mom. You're the one that raised me."

There was a pause. She knew her mother was blinking, trying to keep the tears in her eyes from falling. Her mother did that every time she said something sappy. Well, what her mother would consider sweet.

"Why do you want to know about him?"

"I was just wondering about him," there was a long pause. "I just wanted to know what kind of man he was."

"He was really driven, and worked eighty to nincty hours a week. His every waking moment was how to improve sales, expand the business and make more money. It's been twenty years since he died, and you haven't even wanted to see a picture of him. Now you call out of the blue with questions. What is really going on here?"

Her mother wasn't going to let her off the phone without an answer. She had to come up with something quick, and it had to be something her mother would believe. The fibs rolled naturally. It was kind of scary, but it was what was needed in the moment so she rolled with it. By the time she unlocked the doors for Jason to let into the car, she was hanging up with her mother.

"What's the name of the company your father owns?"

"Cannondale, Inc.," Jason replied as he put on his seatbelt, took the keys back, and started the car. "Why?"

"It seems our fathers worked together until my father died twenty years ago."

Jason put the car back in park, leaned back, and closed his eyes. He looked like he was in shock. She gave him a few seconds to come around to the idea, and then gave him a few minutes. He seemed really thrown by this new information. Finally, she decided she needed to change the subject.

"My mother wanted to know why I'm suddenly interested in my birth father. I told her I met a man and wanted to make sure he wasn't a cousin," she said with a laugh.

"Good thinking." He looked over at her with a grin.

"Yeah, I'd never get her off the phone if I told her the truth. She couldn't be content with the idea of past lives, and not because the evidence doesn't point to that. She doesn't believe in that sort of thing."

His smile faded, and he went back to a pensive expression.

"So, you and I knew each other when we were toddlers, and then after two decades of separation, recognize each other immediately?"

"Not likely," she answered. "The facial differences would be too much, let alone being able to recover a memory from that long ago. And that doesn't explain how you answered those questions."

The silence hung in the car without either of them moving.

"So, where's this lake house?"

Jason laughed. "If there is one, I've never been invited to it." He pulled out his phone and sent a text. They both waited for the reply. "Mom got a kick out of that. No lake house. She said that would require Dad to leave his office." The phone chimed again. He read the text message and laughed. "She said if I find one, let her know. She'd sober up long enough to drive to it."

CHAPTER FOURTEEN

Monica pulled the hem of her skirt down so that it covered her knees. She was in the passenger seat of Jason's car, with the assumption they were headed to church. What else would he have wanted her to dress up for on a Sunday morning? His turn into the golf course was her first indication she might be wrong. Just when she was about to ask where they were going, they passed the sign for the country club, and the large building rose in front of them.

She didn't let her surprise show when he pulled up to the valet parking. Instead, she wrapped her shawl around her shoulders, and thanked the uniformed man that opened her door for her. She smoothed out her skirt as she waited for Jason to come around the back of the car, then fell in step beside him. Two other uniformed young men stepped forward and opened both doors.

Just inside, a man with a jacket and tie matching the uniforms worn outside stood behind a podium. Even though he had a broad smile, she knew he was there to keep the riff raff out; like her. Jason responded to the man's inquiry about his name, and stood there patiently waiting for the employee to look over his paper work. Monica walked over to the glass display case and looked at the trophies. There were also autographed photos of professional golfers. A couple of the names were famous enough for even her to recognize. Most were not.

"Right this way, Mr. Radcliff."

Monica flipped around in surprise. Jason was turned towards her with a big smile. He waited for her before following the man into the restaurant.

"You've got to be shitting me?" She said to Jason just as soon as she was close enough for him to hear her whisper.

He just smiled, pulled her fingers around the bend of his arm, patted her hand once it was in place, and led her through the arch way into the dining area. Even though the room was huge and filled with people, the voices were just a murmur. There was plenty of room for her to walk between the tables without having to turn sideways or brush against the people that she passed. They were led to a table that looked out over the Missouri river with place settings for four.

The waiter pulled her chair out for her. The long table cloth draped over her knees as the chair was pushed forward. She rubbed the material between her fingers, realizing she'd never seen a tablecloth made from material as thick as this. The silver looked genuine, and the glass looked to be crystal. Only once in her life has she had dinner at a place this fancy. All of this for the first meal of the day seemed absurd. The glasses and utensils for two of the place settings were removed from the table.

The waiter walked away. She realized, belatedly, that Jason had spoken to him, and she hadn't heard a word of what had been said. She wanted to ask what she had missed, but he was already hiding behind his menu. She picked up the leather-bound menu in front of her, hoping she would be able to find something on it in her price range. The waiter came back to the table, but didn't say anything before walking away. Confused, she put her menu down.

"Mimosas? Seriously?" She whispered so the people at the other tables wouldn't hear her and pushing the glass away from her. "I don't have the money for this."

"I'm not going to put you in the poor house." He pushed the glass back at her. "It was my idea to come here, I'll pay for it."

She frowned. She hadn't known him very long, but this

didn't seem like him. He was a cold beer, in a recliner, watching the game kind of guy. Yet, he looked just as at ease as everyone else in the room. She was the only one afraid to touch anything.

"Why do you want to spend money like it's water?"

"Because I think it's what we're accustomed to…"

"In this other life?" She finished his sentence.

There was logic to what he said. Since hypnosis was successful, they should be able to spark the memories some other way. So, immersion into the culture did make sense. Monica took a sip of the fizzy drink and was surprised how much she liked it. Once the glass was back on the table, she put her hands in her lap. She realized she was still waiting for someone to deduce that they didn't fit in and ask them to leave. Having been already served a drink, she had to admit that probably wasn't going to happen. She might as well just enjoy the experience. She looked around the room with a new perspective. From the chandelier hanging above them to the real silver silverware, it made the part of her that woke up early expecting nothing but the finest feel right at home.

She didn't want to get used to it, though. The good life had already slipped through her fingers once, she didn't think it was likely she would find it again. She understood Jason's drive to learn everything he could, but she couldn't help but wonder what was going to happen after that. Could she really go back to her tiny apartment and horrible job after knowing what more was out there in the world?

Breakfast was delivered to the table next to them. It looked and smelled delicious. Her stomach suddenly felt empty. She did need to eat, and Jason said he was going to pay for it. She might as well enjoy the experience. Even if nothing else happened, she'd get a good meal out of it.

She thought it was just breakfast at a place she had never tried before. Yet, the little differences were becoming apparent to her. There were no kids running around out of control with parents yelling at them, making the scene even worse. The chair was ergonomically correct, supporting her lower back and making it easier to settle into her surroundings. She did like the place. It was something she really, really could get used to. Despite her own trepidations, she began to hope she could find the life she dreamt about.

When Jason was done with his eggs benedict, he grabbed the Missoulian Sunday edition off an empty table, ordered another mimosa and leaned back in his chair. He seemed more comfortable here than in his own apartment. There were just a few bites left of her omelet and even though she had probably had enough, she couldn't stop picking at it with her fork and putting small bites in her mouth. One bite, that was covered in melted cheese, wasn't so small. She looked up at Jason. Still reading, he folded the paper so it fit better in the small space between him and the table.

Monica gasped, sucking air and the glob of breakfast down her windpipe. Coughing, her body was instinctively trying to remove the foreign object. One hand was on her throat, and the other hand was on the table trying to hold her up through the strong convulsions. Jason put the paper down, rushed over, patted her on the back and encouraged her to keep coughing, instantly understanding that she was choking. Eventually, it did come up without having to resort to the Heimlich Maneuver. As discreetly as possible, she spit the food into her napkin and then sat that on her plate.

"What happened?" Jason asked still kneeling next to her, unconcerned about all the people staring at them.

She tried to talk, but it hurt. He must have seen her cringe in pain, because he handed her a glass. She took a small sip, and the cold did feel good on her throat. She tried another drink, but it was too much, causing just as much pain as it relieved. She put the glass down and tried to talk again. The words came out, but were too hoarse to hear. Instead she picked up the paper, turned it over, and showed him the picture of Clint.

"Oh, shit." He read the engagement announcement, and then handed the paper to her so she could read it also.

Earnest and Barbara Jefferies would like to announce the engagement of their daughter Amanda Maureen Jefferies, who is in her final year at the University of Montana getting a degree in International Relations. She is getting married to Clint Eugene Bower, son of Roger and Mimi Bower, and graduate of UM. The wedding will be in July, after her graduation.

She finally had his full name, though she'd be happy to go back to not knowing it if it meant he wasn't engaged. He was supposed to be *her* fiancé, not this little tart smiling up from the page. It was obvious from the picture she was wealthy, with the clothes and jewelry she wore. How did this girl end up with everything she was supposed to have?

Monica laid the paper down on the table. When she looked up, Jason was staring at her with obvious concern. She tried to smile, but knew it was weak. He smiled in return, only a little bit more believable then hers.

"Do you know Amanda Jefferies?" she asked.

"Not in this life."

"What does that mean?"

"You don't want to hear this right now. You're in shock."

"Yes, I do."

"Fine. She looks vaguely familiar, like she might have been a one night stand. But she's not the type I would be content with having just one time. She's the type I would have pursued."

He didn't have his normal smirk. He was actually being serious.

"You think she's hot?"

"Yep." He shrugged.

"That's not what I want to hear right now," she said.

"I don't tell you what you want to hear. I tell you the truth."

She didn't need to look into his eyes to know he was being straight up with her. It was something she could feel down to her bones. He would never coddle her, but would always be there. Strangely, it reassured her.

"I would like to go now."

He nodded and laid cash down on the table to cover their meal. She stood up, and swayed on her feet. She didn't have to say anything, he was there with an arm around her and helped her out to the car.

◆ ◆ ◆

"Thank you for getting us in so quickly," Jason said walking into the hypnotist's office.

"It's usually a couple days out before I can see someone, but I happened to have a cancellation." Owen motioned them to the same chairs they sat in last time. "So, what can I help you with?"

"We want to try the same thing we did before," Jason said.

"But this time I want to be the one to go under," Monica added.

Owen smiled in response. "I really think what happened last time was a fluke. I doubt we would have anything like that happen again."

"We understand that." Jason leaned back in the chair, getting comfortable. "This would be the same arrangement as we had before; we pay you for an hour of your time, no matter what the outcome is."

The hypnotist clamped his teeth down on his bottom lip and looked back and forth between the two of them. "As long as you're aware I have to do everything I can to keep it mundane and the answers prosaic."

"That's what we're depending on," Monica said. "And I want to remember everything."

She didn't expect both of them to be against her on this, yet they both sat there giving her a disapproving look. Too bad it did nothing to change her mind. "I'm going to make you tell me everything that happens anyway. I might as well remember it and save everyone time."

Owen looked concerned, again. "I don't know if that's the best way to go about this."

"Honey, you were the one worried about false memories clouding our minds. Do you really think it's safe to do that?" Jason asked.

"Having these memories just out of my grasp is already ruining my life. If it pushes me over the edge and makes me officially insane, at least I have a justification for being institutionalized. I already feel like I'm going to be, I might as well know the reason."

Jason nodded in agreement. "These are the questions we want you to ask." He handed over the list they brought with them.

Owen looked like he was going to argue more. He didn't look comfortable with the list, but both Jason and Monica gave him a determined stare, saying they weren't going to do it any other way. "These aren't the vague kind of questions I had in mind."

"We understand that, but the bits of memories that have surfaced have left us with a lot of doubts. We thought, if we knew these couple things, then we might be able to figure the rest out."

Finally, his shoulders sag in defeat and he took the medallion out of the side table. "I want you to focus on the sound of my voice and watch the medallion. Your whole world should focus on those two things. I want you to relax. Clear your mind of all thoughts. My words and the gold circle in front of you is all there is. You feel your eyelids getting heavy."

"Where is the lake house?"

The house was on the east side of Flathead lake. The turn for their road was between two orchards. The dirt road wound down to the water's edge and the house. She also knew what it looked like from the air, when flying in in a helicopter. To answer the question, she rattled off the address.

"When is the wedding supposed to be?"

"June twenty-first," she answered. "The first day of summer."

She could see a table covered in papers, all pertaining to the wedding. There were pictures of orchids that were going to be the center pieces a diagram of the seating assignments, a detailed timeline for the ceremony and reception, and fabric swatches from the bridesmaid's dresses.

"Why was the engagement broke off?" Owen asked.

This question confused her. All she could see was him declaring his eternal love; vowing that nothing would keep them from getting married. Finally, she answered. "It wasn't."

There was a pause. Jason waited for her to explain, but she didn't say anything more.

"What do you do for a living?" Owen read the last question on the list.

"I do a little bit of everything at our father's company, but usually I'm in the think tank. They call me the queen of numbers. I prove everything's possible before we even try it."

When she answered the questions, the information was there without any of the sentiment that went with it. With a snap of his fingers, the delayed emotional reaction washed over her. Her wedding was supposed to be on the longest day of the year, so every year she would have the most time to celebrate their anniversary. Now it was not going to happen. And she still didn't have a reason for it. It was like one day she was engaged, and the next day she was a different person; a single person.

"Just take some deep breaths," Jason said.

Oh, how embarrassing. Both of them were staring at her while she was somewhere between sobbing and hyperventilating. She felt ridiculous, and needed to cam down. Or at least get enough self control to stop making a spectacle of herself. A few deep breaths were enough for Owen to go over to his desk and Jason to stop patting her on the hand.

"Are you okay?" Jason asked.

"I will be." She gave him a fake smile. "It's just a lot to take in."

"So, you got answers?"

She blinked to fight back the tears. "No, not really, but at least I know we didn't break up. For some reason, we just don't know each other anymore."

CHAPTER FIFTEEN

"I can't believe you were able to get the day off," Monica said getting into the passenger seat of Jason's car. He had been waiting at the curb when she walked out of her place.

"Whenever we relocate, we are given a few days off work to help us get settled. I've been able to handle everything on my lunch breaks or in the evening. So, I'm using those days now. Of course, even if I didn't have those, I would have found some way out of the office. Rank has its privileges."

"What does that mean?" She clicked her seat belt in place.

"It means that I'm in charge, so if I decided that I, or everybody that works for me, needs some time off, it happens." He looked over his shoulder, made sure the street was clear, and then pulled out.

"So, you're saying that just because I was able to take some personal time, you would tell everyone in your office to go home for the rest of the day?"

"Yep." He gave her a quick smile and then looked back at the road.

"I wish you were my boss."

"Well, it's not all fun and games. I can be an asshole when I need to be."

He gave her a look she had never seen on him. It was like he took off his nonchalant mask, and revealed the little boy that had been reject by his parents and pushed into a military life at a young age. Then the next second, the mask was back in place and he smiled once more.

"Do you want me to look up the address on my phone?" She had her cell phone in hand.

"Already done." He pulled out folded papers he had tucked next to his seat. "I used my computer to get directions and printed them out."

She took the papers from him and looked them over. The printed-out map showed two routes from Great Falls to Flathead Lake; one looping to the north, and another to the south. There were no roads that would take them straight there. Considering it was only April, and surprise snowstorms could come out of nowhere, it made sense to take the lower route.

"I know my way through town. I'm just going to need to know what turns to make after that and have to help me keep an eye out for signs."

In a block and a half, Jason hit the turn signal. He turned right, merging onto the highway that would carry them west. They talked as he drove. She told him about her co-workers. It was great to hear him laugh at her stories. He had the same twisted sense of humor she did. When that conversation was over, they talked about the things on the side of the road they passed. She didn't know if the endless chatter was making them nervous or giving them an outlet for their tension. Either way, there wasn't a moment of silence for the four hours they drove. They had gone over everything they had discovered so far. Neither of them could come up with anything remotely feasible.

"Maybe it was aliens?" Jason asked.

"What?"

"Maybe we were beamed up into a UFO, and they scrambled our brains?"

"I will admit I'm not an expert on the subject matter, but I'm pretty sure they only experience a loss of memories for the time they're abducted. I've never heard of false memories being added," she said.

When they passed the sign for the orchard, she turned to him to say he needed to turn right at the next road. Before she could get the words out of her mouth, he pushed down on the turn signal. She realized the directions had been discarded at her feet for about ten miles; they hadn't needed them anymore. They were going home.

As they emerged from the just budding fruit trees, they both suddenly stopped talking. It was there, standing in front of them, bigger than life. The lake house was real. She was overwhelmed with relief. Just the sight of it was soothing to her soul.

Which was rapidly followed by a deep feeling of despair. Knowing it was real made her miss it even more than she already had been, and desperate to know why she didn't live there anymore. Jason pulled the car to the edge of the road as they both stared out the windshield with their mouths hung open. The house was three stories and positioned so that two sides of it had views of the lake. The circular driveway led to the large ornate entrance on the uphill side. It was the same view that Jason had drawn in his second sketch, down to the three balconies off the upper floors.

"It's real."

"I feel like I'm home," Jason said in disbelief. "I never felt like I belonged in my parent's house, and it's been more than ten years since I lived there. My whole life I've felt like I've been adrift. But this house I've never seen before feels like home. I'm sure that if I go into that kitchen, I'm going to get my hand slapped for taking something fresh out of the oven."

"Or the empty feeling the house gets when it's the cook's day off and there isn't the aroma of fresh baked goods."

Their eyes met, not needing to say any else. They both nodded in agreement, and sat in silence. It was as if they were taking a moment to mourn all they'd lost. All the chaotic energy from the ride over had been swept away leaving nothing but emptiness in its place.

Their revere was broken when the front door opened. A

petite redhead stepped out and they recognized Amanda Jefferies from her engagement picture. For Monica, all the joy of seeing the house drained out of her. One second everything she wanted sat right in front of her, then she got the reminder she cannot just walk up and take it. It looked like the perfect man came with her dream house. Then, as if in confirmation, Clint stepped out behind her.

The couple talked as Amanda got into her car. Monica grabbed the dashboard, feeling like it was the only thing keeping her from the love of her life. She took a deep breath, reminding herself there were invisible barriers between them; ones she would be harder to get through than just opening the car door and running to him. Just as Amanda was about to close her door, Clint reached down and gave her a peck on the cheek.

"That's the kind of kiss you give a cousin!" Monica exclaimed.

"There's obviously no love in that relationship," Jason said.

Her heart soared, knowing he wasn't in love with the other woman. It had to be a business arrangement. Then, a memory washed over her of being the only one able to draw him away from his work.

"Pull into the driveway. I need to talk to him."

Jason didn't argue. He just put the car in drive and pulled forward as Amanda drove away. Clint was headed back into the house, but stopped when heard the car. He looked back and forth between them as the got out. Monica's heart sank when she didn't see any recognition. She swallowed the lump in her throat and pushed on.

"We need to speak to you."

"I did the announcement in the newspaper already. We aren't interested in any other press coverage."

His baritone voice and the familiar cadence of his words soothed her. If only what he said was as pleasant as how he said it, she might not have a knot of dread forming in her stomach.

"You think we're reporters?" Jason asked.

"It's either that or door to door salespeople, and I'm not interested in that, either."

He didn't know who she was. How was it that she knew him, but he did not know her? That was when it dawned on her that he never really looked at her. He had dismissed them with nothing more than a glance.

"You really don't remember me?" Monica asked, frozen just feet away from him.

Clint looked her over from head to toe and then back up to her face, with a look of boredom and disinterest. "No." He didn't waste time saying anything else. He went inside and closed the door.

She almost collapsed. She had to straighten her legs and lock her knees to keep upright. She pulled air into her lungs and pushed it back out, not sure why she continued to do so. How could he not know her? She knew him before she was even sure he existed.

Her mouth hung open as she stared at the empty porch. That time he had looked at her. It was as if she were a stranger to him. Of all the ways this could have gone, this was the only one she hadn't imagined. And the only one that would leave her devastated. Jason recovered from the shock faster than she did, and tugged her arm to get her back into the car. She stared out the window as they passed one tree after another. Jason stopped at the highway.

"I think we're going about this the wrong way. We need to start with things that are facts now, in this lifetime."

She must have been in shock because her mind was devoid of thought. She had to make herself pay attention to what he said.

"And what are those?"

"That your father and mine used to be business partners. I'll drop you off at your place, and then I'm going to have a talk with my dear old Dad."

"Where is you parent's house?"

"Bozeman."

"What? Wait a second." She turned to face him. "It's completely out of the way to go to Great Falls and then down south."

"Yes. I grasp that. My parents are not the most pleasant people to be around. I wanted to save you that. It's really not an inconvenience to me to take you home first."

"Oh, no you don't." She suddenly felt shock free. "I'm going with you. If he really did know my father, I want to talk to him."

"Okay, but you've been warned."

Jason exited Interstate 90 and took 19th street south. Monica had only passed through on the highway, so she looked out her window, paying attention to what they passed. Retail businesses with large parking lots filled both sides of the road. He drove on for a few miles. They were well south of town before he turned left. One street turned into another. The yards got bigger, and then as they began to climb the houses did, too.

He had what Monica thought of as his 'standing in formation' look; blank face, eyes straight ahead and perfectly still. Well, his eyes were looking around, since he was operating the car, but everything else about him gave off the vibe he was trying to be just another face in the crowd and hope everyone would look past him. She turned her head and watched the scenery, knowing he would talk when he was ready to.

Her mouth fell open when he turned into the driveway. It was a big sprawling house... even larger than the lake house they were just at. It had to be more than five thousand square feet. It was mostly stone. What wood she could see was large exposed support beams. She looked at the other occupant of the car, and realized for him living in the lap of luxury wasn't a pipe dream he woke up with. That was how he was raised, and what he walked away from.

Without saying a word, he got out of the car. She followed his lead. As she closed her door, she could see the valley they had just driven through, and all the lights of Bozeman. To her left, the moonlight highlighted the mountains that surrounded the valley, and a sky teeming with stars capped it all. Jason didn't bother to look at the scenery; he made a bee line for the door.

Eight o'clock seemed late to show up unexpectedly, but there were still lights on and they gave the house an inviting look. That helped calm her nerves. When Jason knocked on the door, she realized the house wasn't inviting at all. If their son had to knock before entering, would anyone get a congenial greeting? Her mother's house was a cottage compared to this place, but she knew it would always be her home. She could come and go as she pleased no matter how long since her last visit.

She wondered if Jason had ever felt wanted in this house. He had lived here as a small child, maybe then? The entire circumstance felt so foreign to her, she took a step back. She wondered if coming along with him had been the right choice. This circumstance was so abnormal for her, would she be able be of any assistance? Then he looked over at her with his cockeyed grin he only gave when the last thing he wanted to do was smile. That was when she realized she might not get anything from the encounter, but she would be there for her friend. She was determined to support him, but hoped she could do so without being noticed by anyone else and stay out of sight behind him.

"Mr. Radcliff." A servant opened the door. "Are you expected this evening?"

She had seen servants act like this on television, but never in real life. Only a couple of the memories she had recovered involved the hired help, but that was just Tess, the cook, who called everyone by their first names.

Jason stepped in, oblivious to the opulence around him. Monica wasn't. Her neck craned up, looking at the chandelier hanging ten feet over their heads. It was the biggest light fixture she had ever seen, with more crystals than she could count. She had no idea what would be over their dinning room table, if this was in the entry way. Her eyes followed the carved bannister back down to the ground, where she was mesmerized by the intricate pattern on the hardwood floor. There were at least three different types of wood used and it must have taken a craftsman weeks to lay it all out.

"No, this wasn't planned," Jason replied. "Are my parents in?"

"I believe your mother has retired for the night. Your father is in his study."

Without a word, Jason headed down the long hallway to the left of the staircase. Monica scrambled to follow him, giving the servant a smile over her shoulder as she did. All she got back was a look of disdain. She turned forward, focusing on the stiff back and long strides leading down the hallway, more than a little shocked that even the domestic help looked down their nose at her. She quickly realized the house was large enough to get lost in and she didn't want to end up wandering from room to room calling out Jason's name. He already had enough on his mind, he didn't need to worry about her, too.

The 'study' was wall to wall bookshelves, spanning from floor to ceiling. It was more than one person could read in a lifetime. She noticed there wasn't a single novel in the entire collection. What was the point in having this many books, if there wasn't any that you could just enjoy?

Heath Radcliff sat behind the large desk to the right, lost in his paperwork. He must have assumed they were just a servant bring something in or taking something out of the room, because he didn't look up. Jason stood there, like he was standing at attention, waiting to be acknowledged. She had the impression this wasn't the first time he waited for his father to notice him.

"Oh, it's you." The father was surprised when he finally glanced up. "You weren't expected. What are you doing here?"

"I just had a couple of questions." He still stood tall, like he could stay that way all night.

"I don't care who you got into trouble, I'm not giving you any money."

Mr. Radcliff was already looking back at the paperwork, like he expected that to end the discussion. She had stepped forward without realizing she had even moved. Her fists were clenched. She looked over at Jason, surprised to see he hadn't moved a muscle. Not even to frown. In fact, he looked bored. She realized as much as she wanted to defend herself, this was Jason's battle. She would let him fight it. She exhaled through pursed lips, took two steps back, and tried to follow Jason's lead.

"If you really have all that money you talk about, maybe you should use some of it to buy hearing aids. All I want from you is a couple of answers, not a favor."

Monica smiled, glad she had refrained from speaking out. The insult was a better response than she had thought of. The older man leaned back in his chair and folded his hands in his lap. He looked up at his son with a scowl.

"Go on."

"What happened to your business partner, Rick Lane?"

Heath was taken aback. It was obvious he was used to knowing what was coming before it happened. He didn't look comfortable answering questions he hadn't had time to prepare for.

"Who is this?"

It seemed he was responding by changing the subject. How unoriginal. She rolled her eyes. Jason still resembled a statue. She should be more like him; if only she were a little more disciplined. Well, that wasn't going to happen, but she could fake it for a few more minutes.

Monica was distracted by the door opening. She expected it to be a servant bringing in refreshments, but instead it was a regal woman with her long blonde hair pulled into a French twist. The resemblance to her son went beyond their identical posture.

"Jason, you came home." Elaine Radcliff breezed into the room and sat down in a high-backed leather chair.

Monica noticed that neither of them had been invited to sit down, and she wasn't going to without being asked. Especially since her friend was still standing. If he stormed out of the room, she wanted to be on his heels when he did.

"This is Monica Lane. Rick's daughter," Jason answered his father's question.

Heath's look of annoyance turned into a look of concern, while his wife looked like her night was just getting interesting. This wasn't the first woman she had met that thrived on drama. Judging the anticipation in the older woman's eyes, she looked forward to the scene that was about to unfold. So much for getting any help from her.

"And how much does she want?" Mr. Radcliff asked.

Monica flipped around to face the old man. Her hand instinctively raised, as if she were fending off a physical blow. She narrowed her eyes at the smug look she got in return. "I don't want any of your money."

The old man's blank stare like he didn't believe her pissed her off.

"It doesn't look like it's made you very happy. My mother has moved on; made a new life for herself. She doesn't like to talk about the past, so when I heard there was someone out there that knew my father, I wanted to talk to them. All I was hoping for was a little connection to a father I never got the chance to know."

Belatedly, Monica remembered she was going to let Jason handle his parents. After all, she was not the one that would have to deal with the consequences. She was supposed to be austere. To her surprise, Jason gave her a nodding approval. He even seemed to have relaxed, a little.

"How is your mother?" Elaine asked.

With a deep breathe, Monica pivoted to face the woman of the house. She knew the question was nothing but a distraction. She welcomed it. Pattering on would give her a few seconds to gather her wits.

"She's good. She invested the money from my father's death into a small house and got her teaching credentials. She teaches science at the junior high school and her new husband teaches English just down the hall from her."

"Oh, that sounds awful," Mrs. Radcliff responded with a scowl.

"My mother's happy with it. She really feels like she's contributing to the world, bringing science into the lives of all those kids."

"She did always want to get involved," the older woman said. "She never could just sit back and enjoy life, like me. What is it that you do?"

"I'm an accountant."

"You took after your father; looking out for yourself, first." The older woman gave her an approving smile.

Monica's composure didn't falter, but the comment struck a nerve. Her mother was a great person, and someone she strived to be like. Had she failed in that? Could she have picked a career field because she was only thinking of herself Maybe that's why she was so miserable. Now wasn't the time, but it was something she wanted to delve into later.

"Your father's death was an accident." Mr. Radcliff said.

"Yes, the police investigation cleared you on any involvement," his wife added.

Monica's head was spinning from all the subject changes. They had succeeded in befuddling her, so Jason respond before she did. "Why were the police looking into it?"

"The detective thought it was suspicious your father called off the merger with Andrew Bower as soon as he found out about the death. They thought he might have murdered his business partner to get out of the deal."

Jason and Monica looked at each other. Andrew was Clint's father. The web was getting more and more tangled with every turn.

"I was in another state, so it was impossible for me to have shoved him over that railing."

Monica knew her father's death had been an accident, but hadn't known the details. Now, she could picture him falling.

"Should I tell the servants to prepare rooms for you?"

Elaine asked.

Monica's mouth hung open. Their diversion tactics finally overwhelmed her. She couldn't keep up with them. The only thing that saved her from screaming was the knowledge Jason was on her side and holding his own.

"No, we're not staying," Jason answered.

"You should know, your father was a damn good business man," Heath finally seemed to let some of his resentment go. "I didn't agree with him about the merger, but he did a great job of setting up the company with me. I've been doing the work of two ever since just to keep it running."

Finally, something was said about her family that wasn't condescending; just when she'd given up hearing anything decent. It took the edge off her bitterness, but didn't remove it completely.

"Did you ever think that if you'd gone through with the merger you would have had someone to share the workload with?" Monica asked.

"Pretty thought," the older man responded. "Bower's even more driven than Rick was. I was tired of being badgered into taking the company in directions I didn't want to go, and took his death as a sign that I shouldn't. I would rather fail my way than succeed under someone else's leadership. And as you can see around you, I haven't failed." He was a stubborn, proud man that wasn't going to change his opinions.

It seemed Jason had come to the same conclusion. When they locked eyes, she could see some of the weariness. She got a quick smile before his mask was back in place.

"Thanks for the warm reception." Jason swept out of the room, with Monica lengthening her strides to stay right behind him.

CHAPTER SIXTEEN

The tires squealed pulling out of the driveway. "I'm sorry."

"For what?" Monica asked, truly not knowing why he had made that comment.

"I thought we would be able to find something out, instead of my parents playing their usual games."

"We did find things out. I got to know more about my Dad."

Jason shook his head. "I hoped we would have another breakthrough and discover more about our memories."

She didn't say anything; instead just stared off out the window. She couldn't think of the right thing to say, so she said nothing at all.

"I've been thinking about it, and I think we can do the hypnotism ourselves, without Owen." He interrupted the silence.

She looked down at her watch; it was almost nine at night. "If we're going to try it, I think we should stop and get a hotel."

He flashed the first big smile she had seen in hours. "Great minds think alike."

Once they were back in town, they had a many of hotels to choose from. Monica had no preference on where they stayed, so she sat quietly while he found them a place that looked comfortable. He parked the car in the first empty spot he found.

"I don't want you to worry about money, I will pay for your room."

With everything that had just happened, money was the last thing on her mind. She nodded, knowing he was just as tired as she was. "Um, I'd rather share yours, if you don't mind."

His big toothy grin was his answer. She smacked him in the arm, "Not like that. A room with two beds. You sleep in yours and I'll sleep in mine. I have a hard enough time figuring out where I am when I wake up in my own bed, I can't imagine what it will be like in a hotel. If you're there, it might help."

"Anything for a damsel in distress." He got out of the car.

She rushed out after him. "It's a waste of time flirting with me,"

"You act as if I have control over it. I can't open my mouth without something teasing coming out of my mouth." He looked down at her as they strode towards the entrance.

"That time you didn't even have speak. Your smile was more than enough."

"My powers are getting stronger." When she frowned, he nudged her in the shoulder and added. "I promise it's nothing personal, it's how I talk to everyone."

She knew he spoke the truth and could remember another lifetime of laughing at his cheesy come-ons. He flamboyantly opened the door for her, motioning her in with his arm. She couldn't help but smile at him. Once inside, she stepped to the side. Since he was paying, she let him do all the talking. While he handed over his credit card and driver's license, she wandered around the lobby. There was a sign about the continental breakfast. Her stomach growled, reminding her they missed dinner. She wouldn't be able to wait until morning to get food.

"Is there somewhere we can get something to eat."

"The restaurant across the street is closed by now. There is a pizza place open late, that delivers out here."

The desk clerk handed her a paper with the list of nearby places to eat. The pizza joint was at the top of the list. Jason held up the room key cards.

"All done. Room 412." He thanked the front desk clerk and led the way to the elevators.

"Peperoni and olives all right with you?" She asked exiting the elevator and following the signs to their room.

"If you add some mushrooms with that."

She nodded. Mushrooms weren't her favorite, but she didn't mind eating them. He unlocked the door and let them into the room. As soon as she was through the door, her cell phone was out. She dialed the top number and told them she wanted delivery.

"What is the address."

Crap. "Hold on a second."

She had forgot all about needing the address. There had to be something in the room with it. She went over to the desk and went through the papers. There was a binder, listing the services they offered. She found exactly what she was looking for on the cover page. She read it out loud and put in her order.

"That will be about thirty minutes."

"Thank you."

By the time she was done, Jason had the television on and was stretched out on the far bed. She moved up all the pillows on the other bed to the side closest to the night stand, and reclined there.

"I think we remember another timeline," Monica said.

"What do you mean, another timeline?"

"I think we lived one life where that merger went through and we grew up together. Then something happened, and all that changed. Now we're are in another time line, one that doesn't seem to have worked out as well for us."

"You think someone traveled through time and changed our lives." He had completely turned to face her, with his legs hanging off the side of the bed. The disbelief not only filled his tone, but showed in his expression as well.

"It's the only thing that makes any sort of sense."

"Other than the fact that time travel is impossible, that

makes perfect sense." He rolled his eyes.

"None of what's happening makes sense. We've looked at it from every angle. There isn't a rational explanation. The only option we have left is to look at the irrational."

He didn't respond right away. He looked like he finally took her suggestion seriously and was giving it real thought.

"One thing I don't understand is why are we the only people that remember anything from the other timeline?"

"Because we're the only ones unsatisfied with how things turned out?"

That made sense to her. Her mother was genuinely happy, and that wasn't something she had seen in what little bit she remembered of the other time line. As far as his parents, she didn't understand their lifestyles, but they both seemed content with it. That made her wonder about Clint. Was he overjoyed with the new woman in his life? She didn't want to consider the answer could be anything other than no. But she had to admit, of all of them, his life had changed the least. He still lived in the same house, worked the same job, and was still engaged.

"Well, until I see the time machine, I'm not going to believe it. And I don't see one here in the hotel room. How do you propose we find it?"

"Hypnosis." She slid two fingers under the neck line of her shirt. A gold locket slipped over the collar of her tee-shirt. She undid the clasp, and handed it to him. "My step-father gave it to me the day he proposed to my mother. He said that even though he hoped to be there for me the rest of my life, he would never try to replace my father. Inside is a picture of my real Dad, and my baby picture."

Jason opened the locket. "I can see the resemblance, but fortunately you got most of your looks from your mother." He flashed her another smile, to go along with the obvious pick-up line. He was never going to change. Then she smiled, reassured that he would, in fact, always stay the same.

With a little shift of his wrist, the necklace started swaying. "I want you to relax. Focus on me and the sound of my voice." He paused, giving her time to take a deep breath. "We are the only ones here, and I'm here for you through all of this." He added another moment of silence, keeping the pace slow and relaxing. "I just want you to relax, so we can talk about this." She closed her eyes and she shoulders sagged. "I want you to describe an average workday to me."

"At the lake house, or in the city?" she asked.

"What city?"

"Missoula." She could see the mountains surrounding the city, and the Clark Fork River winding through downtown. In the middle of summer, they would float down the river on inner tubes.

"You have an office in Missoula?"

"We all have offices in the corporate building. We are being groomed to take over the company from our parents."

"Parents?"

"I know Mrs. Radcliff and Mrs. Bower don't actually work there, they do volunteer work, but I figure four out of six is enough to clump them all together."

"Your mother works for the company?"

"Yes, she works in product development... with you." The image that popped into her head was of her mother waiving good bye as she was about to go into the lab.

"What's the company's name?"

"Crowne-n-Dale."

"Tell me about the days you work from the lake house."

An image of the lake house appeared in her mind, but was quickly replaced by a metal pole barn. It had a large gravel parking lot and she always used the spot right in front of the window. Inside were two desks, a few work benches, a huge tool chest and at the back a maze of shelves filled with everything they might possibly need to create something never seen before.

"I do the structural mechanical analysis. I come up with the mathematical equations to prove if a concept will work or not."

"So, you can do that from anywhere?"

"Exactly, which means it's convenient for me to join Andrew in his workshop."

"What workshop?"

"The barn," she answered. "That's what we called it as kids, anyway. It's a big steel building out in the middle of a field. We also call it the 'think tank', since that's where we make the prototypes."

"Do you like what you do?"

"I love it. I'm on the cutting edge of technology. I'm making the future."

"I'm going to have you wake up now. I want you to remember everything we talked about. On the count of three you'll open your eyes and be alert. One. Two. Three." He snapped his fingers.

Being a little disoriented, she had to close her eyes. While under hypnosis, she felt content for the first time in years. It was more than that, the other her was happy and thought the world was a great place. Her career, her whole life, inspired her and filled her with joy. It immediately rushed out of her as she remembered a life of adding columns of numbers and chasing receipts, but she tried to hold on to some of that feeling. She opened her eyes, and blinked at the bright lights. Everything was the same as it had been, except Jason had his phone, out.

"What are you doing?"

"You said that you worked for Crowne-n-Dale Corporation. I was just looking up the name, but there are no corporations with that name in Montana or any other place. I did find information on a Crowne, Incorporated ran by Andrew Bower."

Jason answered the door and took care of paying for the pizza, giving her a few more minutes to sort everything out in her head. She heard the door close, and then he turned the corner with the iconic large square box balanced on his hand. The aroma hit her, and she could lay there no longer. She jumped up and met him at the table. He opened the lid, and she snatched up the piece closest to her. When he handed her a napkin, she realized grease ran down her hand. With her mouth full, she said thank you and wiped up the mess. They both flopped down on chairs, unwilling to get more than arms reach away from the food. Monica reached over to grab another slice and found nothing but cardboard.

"We've both had four slices, should I order another one," he asked.

She had eaten so fast, she didn't know how full she was until she stopped. Suddenly, her stomach was uncomfortable.

"No. I don't need any more. Did you get enough?"

He rubbed his belly. "I'm good. So, you want to try doing me?"

She looked over at him, expecting this to be one of his tongue-in-cheek come-ons, but he looked completely serious. He had to mean hypnosis. Just thinking about it made her tongue tied.

"I'm going to need a moment to look this up. I need something to tell me what to say, I can't improvise this."

Jason went over to the bed and propped himself up on the pillows like he had been before. He had a remote in hand, and looked comfortable. She went back to her scrolling, clinked on a link and found exactly what she was looking for. Her locket was still on the nightstand. When she picked it up, he turned off the television, put the remote down and started to get up.

"Actually, it says you should stretch out and get comfortable."

She sat down on her bed, facing him with her legs dangling off the side. The website stressed that she needed to be tranquil in order for it to work. She took a few deep breaths, and realized he was watching her. She smiled.

"I need you to be at ease. We are going to start with your feet. Focus on them. Fan out your toes and then let them curl back up. Feel all the tension seep out of the muscles."

She had him work all the way up his body, working each group of muscles as they went. His eyes were closed, and he looked serene.

"Now that you're calm, I want you to bring your attention to your breathing." She slowly said. "Take a deep breath. As you let it out, begin to feel yourself relax once more."

She could hear his slow, deliberate respirations. When she wasn't talking, it was the only thing in the room.

"I want you to concentrate on each inhale and each exhale as you let yourself sink even deeper into a trance."

She realized they hadn't discussed what they would talk about once he was under. She was at the end of her script, and didn't know what to say next. Since he didn't give her any guidance, she was free to satisfy her own curiosity.

"How long have you known Clint?"

"I was three or four when we met, or so I'm told. I don't actually remember. It's like he's always been a part of my life."

"And you like him?"

"He's my best friend, and my future business partner. I know sharing a company may not mean much to other people, but to me, to all three of us, it means more. When the two corporations merged, it somehow became a family business. We picked up what our parents created, and are making it bigger than they ever imagined it could be. I've taken it to three continents. Clint understands everything in my life. I can turn to him about anything and he understands, because he has the same background and the same goals."

"And what's our relationship?" The question rolled off her tongue before she realized what she was asking. She should have, at least, worded it better.

"The same as I have with Clint," he answered. "You're the other leg of the tri-pod. I would say you're like my little sister, but that's not quite right. I see you more like an equal. It's like separate we're just line segments, but together we're a scalene triangle."

"How did the lake house become so important to us?"

"You are the reason we all started going there. It was a Thursday dinner, and all nine of us were at the table. Mimi announced that she wouldn't be able to host the next weeks dinner, because she was going to take Clint to her family home on

Flathead Lake for spring break. You yelled out that she couldn't do that. Everyone looked at you in surprise, and you crossed your arms and stared back. You were so small, only in the first grade, the defiant gesture just looked cute.

"Mimi calmly asked you why you said that. You explained that when you agreed to go to that stuffy old Catholic school, it was because you were promised you would be able to see the boys during vacation. You had done your part, and gone to that icky school, so now you deserved to spend spring break with Clint.

"Everyone laughed, which made you scowl even harder. So, Mimi invited you to come up to the lake house with them. We all expected you to turn to your parents and ask their permission to go. Your lips puckered before say, 'But that's only half. I would get to see Clint, but not Jason'.

"Your Dad told you that was just life. Things didn't always work out the way you wanted them to. Your lips started quivering, and we were sure you were going to start crying. Mimi jumped in and said that you were right; everyone should come up for Easter weekend, and Elaine and the kids were welcome to stay the rest of the week when everyone else needed to get back to work."

The more he talked, the more she remembered the summers they all spent at the lake. She remembered counting down everyday of the school year until she got to see the boys again.

CHAPTER SEVENTEEN

When Monica woke up to the sound of the shower, she knew she wasn't home... or if on the really weird chance she was, she wasn't alone. She opened her eyes to find she was fully dressed laying on top of a still made hotel bed. The one across from her was still made too, with just a few creases to indicate it had been slept upon. They must have fallen asleep while they were both talking.

Her purse was on the dresser. She made her way over, and dug through it until she found her phone. She wanted to call out sick from work while she still had the gravelly, morning voice. No one answered, so she left a message.

Inhaling the aroma of coffee, she realized the shower wasn't making all the sounds she heard. There was a coffee pot percolating next to the sink. She washed her face, and by the time she was finished, the coffee was done. It was a small pot, so she poured half of it into her cup, leaving the rest for Jason. He stepped out fully dressed in the clothes he wore the day before. The only sign he had bathed was his still damp hair.

"Do you want to jump in the shower?"

"It seems silly when I have to put the same clothes back on."

He shrugged and poured himself the rest of the coffee. "Then we can get on the road right away."

"Where are we going?"

He turned around, leaned against the counter, and took

a leisurely sip of his coffee. He knew she was waiting for him. When he lowered his cup, he was smiling. "The barn."

She almost dropped her coffee, spilling a little on the carpet before she got a secure hold on it.

"That's up by the lake house, like five hours from of here. We just got here *from there*. Now you want to turn around and go back?"

"Yep." He shrugged, drank what was left of his coffee and then threw away the disposable cup. "That's where the clues point, so that's where I'll go. Besides, you're going to calling out sick from work, what else do you have to do today?"

"You're such a pompous ass."

"Thank you."

She had started to walk away, but turned back around. "That was not a compliment."

"Maybe to you it wasn't, but that doesn't mean that I don't get to think it is."

She shook her head and finished walking over to the desk. She slid her phone inside her purse.

"What do you think we're going to find there?"

"A big metal building in the middle of a field."

She laughed, rolled her eyes, and then finished looking around the room, making sure she didn't leave anything. Being that everything she had with her was already over her shoulder, there was nothing to leave behind. "I will need breakfast, even if it's something we get from a drive-thru."

Most of the way, they were just back tracking on the same roads they took the day before. Unlike the previous day, neither of them felt the need to fill the silence. Most of the time, Monica sat with her head rolled to the side watching the scenery go by.

"I can remember what the barn looks like, but I'm still a little fuzzy on how to get there." Jason said.

Maybe it was because she had pulled up the memories

under hypnosis, or because she spent more time working there in the other life, but she was able to see every turn in her head.

"As we drive up Highway 35, instead of turning left towards the lake make a right turn up hill."

"This is weird. Once you say it, I can picture it and know it's right."

It was a long, open road leading to the work shop, so they were able to see it clearly in the distance as they drove up. They remembered it being blue, but what little paint was on the building was white. Most it was bare metal siding with rust. The yard was just as neglected; over grown and dead.

"Well, Andrew's car is parked in its normal spot." Monica said.

"That's all that's the same."

"Let's hope it's not the *only* thing."

The car lumbered into the parking lot over bumps that hadn't been there before. She was jostled so hard, her head smacked the window.

"Sorry," he said. "I drove in like I used to, not realizing the weeds grown up in the gravel are covering up ruts."

"It's okay." She rubbed her head.

She got out of the car and looked up at the large steel building towered in front of them, with two large garage doors on the left and a man-sized door on the right. She went to the small door, knowing that side of the building had his computer work station and his shop tools. He might not be able to hear her knock if she went to the other side.

Her hands went for the knob. She clenched her fist at her side to keep from letting herself in, like in all of her memories. A little knot of fear formed in her belly, and she wasn't so sure she wanted to know what was on the other side. With a deep breath, she banged her knuckles on the white metal.

The door only opened a crack, it was so dark inside she could only see the eyeball peering out at her. Then the door was flung open, two large arms seized her and she was pulled inside. "Monica, where have you been!"

She felt Jason grabbed the back of her shirt and yank her back outside. She was getting thrown around like a rag doll. Jason came around her with his fist up, ready to attack whomever had tried to hurt her. Digging her heels into the ground, she stopped her backwards momentum. Then propelled herself up, latching on to his arm that was about to strike and used all her weight to pull it down.

"Jason, you're here, too." Andrew Bower exclaimed, not understanding he almost got hit. "Come in quick and lock the door behind you. We have a lot work to do."

The old man assumed they were doing as they were told and disappeared inside the shop.

"He wasn't trying to hurt me."

The soldier nodded. His arms were at his sides, fingers relaxed, but his eyes still jumped around. "Got it. It was just a reflex reaction. I'm fine now."

They stepped forward, but upon seeing the interior, stopped just inside the door. She heard the door being locked behind her. The shop she had been meticulous about keeping clean was a disaster. Every horizontal surface was covered with tools, parts, and garbage. She frowned knowing it would take her a week to put everything back where it belonged.

There was a white board next to the desk with a long mathematical equation on it. This is what she did; what she loved. Anyone could add up columns of numbers, she wanted to work with theoretical science. The formula on the board wasn't familiar to her; she hadn't seen it any lifetime.

"I'm so glad you guys are here," the older man said as he gathered different items from all over the shop. "This will all go so much faster with extra hands. Not to mention the additional brain power. With your combined intelligence added, there's no way we can't solve this."

"Mr. Bower, you remember us?" Jason asked.

The question made the grey-haired man stop in his tracks. He halted so fast, the pile of parts in his arms shifted and one of them fell at his feet. He didn't seem to notice the chunk of metal that came less than an inch from hitting his toe.

"Of course, I know you," he said, blinking a couple times. "Don't you remember me? You must recollect something, or you wouldn't be here. Nobody comes to this place by accident."

"The life we remember doesn't include you," Monica explained stepping forward. "The life with you in it is only a dream. We've had random bits of memories we've had to connect."

Andrew dumped everything in his arms onto the table in front of him, rushed over to where she was standing, and clutched her upper arms with a smile. "If anyone could put together the pieces, it would be you."

"I couldn't have done it without Jason."

"And he was with you, in this other life?" His head swung back and forth, waiting to see which would answer.

"Not with me," Monica said.

"Ran into her at the bank. We recognized each other at first sight."

"In the new timeline, you didn't know each other and still there was recognition when your path's crossed. Amazing."

"Mr. Bower, you only remember the old timeline, don't you?" Monica asked.

"Yes." The old man's eyes dropped to the floor. "Since I was outside the space-time continuum when the shift happened, I wasn't a part of it. I didn't get any of the new memories."

"What do you mean you were outside the space-time continuum?" Jason asked.

"Einstein's space-time continuum is most often represented as fabric that's spread throughout the universe. I like to think of it as a trampoline, and the Earth as a bowling ball dropped on its surface. The fabric bends around the surface of the ball/Earth..."

"What does that have to do with..." Jason interrupted.

"Patience my boy, I'm getting to that," The older man shook off the cut in and started pacing. "Like I was saying, the space-time continuum bends around the Earth, so I went inside the planet. Here on the property is an old gold mine that goes deep under a mountain mainly composed of quartz that hasn't been used in more than a century. I bought this place long ago with the theory time travel might be possible there, but I never had the nerve to try it before. But now... since I had nothing to lose, I pulled out my old research. Using electromagnetic rails, three of them in circles to make an orb, I created an artificial space-time continuum deep below the Earth's surface."

Both of the younger people stood in shock.

"By using a short, controlled burst, I was able to determine which direction accelerated faster than the continuum on the surface and which direction went backwards. I figured out a calculation to show the amount of power used multiplied by the time it's applied in seconds equals the amount of time that's passed on the surface."

"Why," Jason asked. "What was so dire that you resorted to this?"

"Rick..." Mr. Bower said mid stride.

"My Dad?" She gasped, sure he had to mean someone else. It was a common name.

"Yes." He stopped pacing to stand in front of her. "Your father betrayed us all; the company, your mother, and you. He stole our new products that were about to be revealed, and ran off with his secretary."

"So, you went back in time and killed him?" she asked, taking a step back, away from him.

Suddenly she was sure coming here had been a huge mistake. What had she been thinking? All of this happened so fast, it felt like a game. In an instant, everything seemed too real, and they might have ensconced themselves in with a killer.

"No." He stepped forward, closing the distance between them and gathering her hands in his. "He was alive when I left him. You have to believe me. He was guilty of corporate espionage. He sold out secrets to our competitor and used the money to run off with his secretary. I went back to reason with him. The other company had the defense contracts, but they couldn't produce the goods. If we just waited them out, they would lose the contract and then we can prove that we can produce what they weren't able to.

"Something went wrong," Andrew continued and went back to pacing. "I thought I had gone back two years, but ends up I had gone back twenty. It's hard to scare someone away from destroying a company when it hasn't been created yet. I decided to take another tactic. Since he was so interested in self-gratification, I dangled what I knew like a carrot in front of him. I told him we did get the contract, but told him he would succeed when I had actually failed in real life. I was so excited to see if a mere suggestion could really change the outcome, I raced back here, both to my property and our time."

She thought back to everything she knew about the other timeline, more specifically about her Dad and Andrew. Unfortunately, she hadn't uncovered much about either. The only image she had for her father was him sitting in his office. The only conversation she could recall was about a work project. Memories about Andrew came easier. They had spent most of their time working together in the shop. He was a kindred spirit, understanding that mathematics was its own language. Never, in any of the memories, had she had any reason to mistrust him. Her friend was beside her, gripping her shoulder. She patted his hand. "It's okay. I know he didn't do it on purpose."

Monica wondered to the white board. "Is this the equation?"

"Yes," the fatherly man answered.

The room was silent as she stared at the board. The meaning of each symbol flew through her head. She could see all the ways they worked together. One part of the equation stood out to her as not connecting with the rest.

"This part of the equation is wrong." She paused mid-sentence. "If you use the cube root... I can fix this."

Hands on her upper arms swung her around before she could reach the marker. When she came to a stop, Jason was just inches from her with the same expression he had when he almost hit the other man.

"No, you can't. Don't fix it, because it can never be used again. This time your father died. You're stuck in a miserable existence balancing someone else's check book for a living and I'm in the Air Force. What do you think is going to happen if another trip is made? Anything you try will have unforeseen consequences. We could end up dead, for all you know."

"You're right," she said with a frown. "I just got caught up in the realization I could do it."

Mr. Bower turned to the younger man. "I realized everything was wrong as soon as I got back. I no longer knew half the people in my company. My own son seems like a stranger to me, and his fiancé..." His eyes darted to Monica. "was not who I expected. My wife thinks I'm staying up here to protest my own son's wedding."

That was why her engagement was off. With everything unfolding, she hadn't made the connection until he said something. It was reassuring to know she hadn't been dumped, even if she didn't know what she was going to do about it.

"That was when I learned that your father had died. He was a smart man. I think he figured out I was from the future. I hadn't thought about the fact I obviously look older than the Andrew Bower he'd been having business meetings with. He must have chased after me, wanting to know how I had come back in time. He lost his balance and fell from the second floor just minutes after I left. I've spent the last two weeks in a stand still. Do I go back and attempt to undo what I changed, or will that just create another paradox that I can't even begin to imagine?"

Jason had his I-told-you-so look. No one responded to it.

"There has to be another way to fix this." Monica said.

"Can we fix the time line discrepancies from now, without going back?" Jason asked.

"I don't know." Andrew scratched his head while he thought about it. "In this reality, Crowne Corporation has the defense contracts, but I no longer have the technology to fulfill them."

"Well, you said it was just a matter of time before we'd have the contracts. Let's go with the assumption it would have happened in either time line, we've just accelerated it a little in this one," Monica said. "We just need to put our heads together and reinvent the equipment."

"If we bring your mother in…" Mr. Bower started.

"No," Monica snapped.

Both men turned to her in surprise.

"I mean…well…I just." She finally stopped stammering and took a few breaths. "My mother is really happy. She has a man that loves her, and a career she considers fulfilling. In all the memories of the other time line, I can't recall her smiling once. I just remember her being driven. I don't want her brought back into this life, especially not to a husband that left her for a younger woman."

"I don't think we need her," Jason spoke up. "I think between the three of us, and our memories of the other timeline, we can rebuild everything."

Andrew looked like what he heard was too good to be true. "Do you think we could really pull it off?"

Jason offered a big smile that left no room for doubt.

"I quit." Monica said to her boss over the phone.

"What?" The older man said. "What do you mean?"

"I know this is not how it's usually done. I would do this in person and give you two weeks' notice, but something unexpected came up that has taken me out of town. I don't know when I will be back."

She was pacing outside the barn, having had assumed this would go much smoother. She thought she was just going to say 'I quit' and have that be the end of the conversation.

"We understand family emergencies. We can pause your employment for as long as you need. No rush. You've been a great employee, so we won't leave you out in the cold. All we ask is that you give us updates on when you will return."

"Thank you for the offer. I really appreciate it. Unfortunately, I don't when, if ever, I'm going to come back. I would feel guilty if I gave you false expectations. Have a good day, Mr. Morris."

She ended the call before he could say anything else. Already, she was filled with doubt, but something inside her felt like there was no going back. Even if this job didn't come to fruition, she refused to go back to one she hated. She might as well make the break now.

Jason stepped out into the warm sunshine. "Andrew and I agree the first thing we need to do is recover the lost memories, so we can get the details about all of our designs. He's going to take us to the lake house so we can be comfortable enough to do it."

She tingled with excitement. She was going to the house of her dreams... and gets to go inside. Andrew came out, fumbling with his pockets.

"I know I have keys here, somewhere."

When his hand came out of his jacket pocket, it jangled. The lock took a moment to secure, then he turned back around and smiled.

"We'll follow you over." Jason said.

"That's good. That's good." Mr. Bower said going over to his car.

Monica shadowed Jason, getting into his passenger seat. "He seems really frazzled, doesn't he?"

"The old man?" Jason started the car and carefully backed it out onto the road. "Yeah, but he already seems better than when we first got here."

"I think so, too. I just worry about the toll all this has taken on him."

"There's not much we can do about that. Our only option is to look forward and find solutions."

He was right. Stressing about it wasn't going to help anyone. The section of road they were travelling on was thick with trees with branches that grew over the pavement. She suddenly had a memory of calling it a tunnel when she was a small child. The adults in the vehicle corrected her; pointing out there was sky poking through the green. Jason and Clint were in the back seat with her. When they looked up, all they could see was the roof of the car. They instantly started whispering, deciding their parents were wrong, and this was the secret tunnel between the house and the shop.

The garage door rose when they pulled into the driveway. Andrew parked inside, while Jason parked off to the side of the building. The home owner waited next to his car when they walked up to the still open rolling door.

"This way," was all the man said before turning around and heading towards the far door. There were spaces for two other vehicles that weren't occupied. The only other thing in the garage was the old pick-up truck that rarely left the house.

The door led directly to the kitchen. The smell of fresh baked bread enveloped them, just like in their memories. Tess, the cook, was on the far side of the butcher block island peeling potatoes. Images flooded her mind of Tess. In some of them she had brown hair, and in other's she had the silver that currently was wrapped in a bun. The hair style was always the same, even if the color had changed.

"These two will be joining me for dinner," Mr. Bower instructed.

"Is there any food allergies or intolerances I need to be aware of?"

The nostalgic feeling stopped with the reminder they were guests. Instead, she suddenly felt alone and out of place. The woman that was so familiar to her, didn't recognize her at all. She knew that odors were closely linked with memory, and that was what was causing her to have an emotional reaction.

"I'm allergic to strawberries," Jason said.

"I don't have any dietary restrictions," Monica added.

"Do I assume that means you won't be dining in your

quarter's again?"

The old man frown and shook his head at her flippant remark. "No. We will be working in the study, so you can serve us there. Oh, they will be sleeping in the east wing. Can you make sure the heat is turned on?"

"Is your luggage outside?" Tess asked.

"Oh, we don't have anything." Monica responded.

"Very well. The housekeeper is still here. I'll have her make sure those bathrooms are stocked with the essential toiletries." The chef went back to what she was doing.

They were being dismissed from the kitchen. Monica didn't have any specific memory to support the feeling, but she knew it all the same. It did make sense; the woman had to suddenly triple whatever she was making.

The swinging door led them out to the main hallway. It was the same carpet over the same gleaming hardwood floors she remembered. Familiar paintings hung on the walls. Andrew led them into a room with ceiling to floor book shelves on all four walls. Monica went directly to where her favorite books were shelved, but none of them were there. Of course, she had never bought them in this timeline. A desk stood askew on the other side of the room, taking up one corner of the Persian rug. Comfortable, high back chairs circled the rest of it.

"So, what do you need?" The aging scientist sat down in the first chair to the right.

"Just my locket," Monica said as she took it off.

The rest of the afternoon was spent with Jason or her in a trance, reciting every detail they could recover about the shop and everything that had been made there.

CHAPTER EIGHTEEN

"Dad, I brought those contracts you wanted, but I don't know what you need them for. We don't have any positions open at corporate," Clint said as he walked into the barn.

"I'm not hiring anyone for the main office," Mr. Bower answered from the back of the shop. "I'm hiring a staff for here; in the think tank."

"You're the only one that calls it that," the son retorted. "All you do is tinker here."

Monica worked at the white board, just behind where Clint stood. Even though she knew he was coming, seeing him was still a shock. He had just had a haircut and the back of his neck was freshly shaved. She wanted to reach out and caress the smooth skin. Clint turned around, and then jumped when he saw her.

"What the Hell." He had a hand on his chest and was breathing rapidly. "I wasn't expecting anyone else to be here."

His eyebrows bunched up as he looked up at her. "You're the woman that was at the house the other day."

His scowl was more than she could bear. Her lower lip quivered, and it was suddenly a struggle to draw in air. Mr. Bower and Jason emerged from behind a large piece of machinery. Clint swung around at the noise.

"Oh, and her boyfriend is here, too."

"He's not my boyfriend."

"I'm not her boyfriend." They both answered at the same time.

This wasn't the man she knew. He looked the same, and dressed the same, but this man obviously didn't trust anyone. He was so quick to assume the worst. She started to question if this really was the man she was in love with.

"Son, this isn't what you think it is."

"And what do I think it is, Father?"

The old man sighed. "I don't know what's going through your head, but I know you don't have all the facts. So, whatever conclusions you've arrived at can't be right."

"You haven't told him?" Monica stepped up. No wonder he was freaked out. He had no idea what was going on. Now, she understood why he was on edge.

"I tried. He wouldn't let me," Mr. Bower explained.

"So, you can't bother to come to my engagement party, but you can open up to these two complete strangers."

"They are here to try and help me fix everything."

"They don't look like doctors," Clint retorted.

"Doctors?" Monica stepped over to the fatherly man. "Are you okay?"

"I'm fine, child." He patted her hand. "He think's I've developed Alzheimer's."

Grinning, Monica said "I bet he would."

Clint's eyes narrowed, not liking being laughed at. "In the last two weeks you've suddenly forgot the most basic things about your life. What was I supposed to think?"

No one answered. Clint looked around at each of them, challenging them to respond. When no one did, he pulled the contracts out of his briefcase and set them on the table in front of him. "If hiring you a couple of assistants will help, let's get this over with. What's your name?" He looked to his left.

"Monica Lane."

He wrote down her response at the top of the form. "And what do you do for a living?"

"I'm an accountant."

Clint capped the pen without writing anything and looked up at his father. "You already have a bookkeeper that does your personal finances."

"She's a mathematician." The old man tapped the papers and gave him a stern look like the subject wasn't open for debate.

"And how much will their salaries be?" Clint had moved down to the next blank on the form.

"They will each make two hundred and fifty thousand a year, and that will double after two years," Mr. Bower said with the same tone indicating he didn't expect any backtalk.

"That's some high paid assistants," Clint mumbled as he wrote the figure down. Then he looked to his right. "And you are?"

"Jason Radcliff."

"Any relation to Heath Radcliff?" The younger Bower asked.

"He's my father."

"Corporate espionage?" Clint threw the pen down on the paper. A black line appeared where it slid across. His eyes narrowed on his father and his face turned red. "Is that what we've been reduced to?"

"How can it be espionage when I've never worked for my father?"

"But you've lived in the same house as him. You've been privy to what's going on in his company," Clint argued.

"Not since I was twelve," Jason responded. "Then I was too young to understand anything I might have heard, and it was all too long ago for me to remember, anyway. The only conflict that exist with me is my current commitment to the United States Air Force. I'm prepared to resign my commission, but refuse to do so without a contract. I'm not about to throw all my eggs in one basket without making sure the basket will hold."

Clint looked around the room, "What is going on here?"

"I think it's time you told him," Monica said to Mr. Bower.

◆ ◆ ◆

"The proof is in the pudding," Andrew said as he motioned them all into the mine.

Only two of the helmets had attached lamps. Monica was wearing one of them. She wanted to argue that she didn't need it, but there seemed to be a consensus among the men that she would have it. She didn't waste her breath with rebuttal; not three against one. Mr. Bower had the other one. He said he needed his hands to operate the equipment.

Little was said as they trekked down through the tunnel. She watched as all four of their lights bounced off the walls in erratic patterns. She had been right about the time travel, and now she was going to see the proof. She was so excited, she bounced as she walked. They had been underground about twenty minutes when they made it to the machine. The elder Bower went around the cavern turning on the work lights. They saw that the area had been turned into a make shift mechanical space, with power and hand tools scattered around.

"Is seeing believing?" she asked, nudging Jason.

"I'd already been convinced," he admitted.

Clint glared at both of them. "Well, I haven't."

Sighing, she looked over at the young executive. She wanted to help the man she loved. It took everything she hadn't to reach out to him. The daggers he shot her with his eyes make it obvious he didn't want to be touched.

The sound of spinning magnets filled the cavern. They all turned around to the machine that sitting in the corner. It was silent. Suddenly an identical machine appeared in the center of the mine. They all turned to the older man.

"What's happening?"

"I have to admit, I'm just as confused as you all are," the older man replied. "I haven't touched anything. At least, not yet."

"What do you mean, not yet?" Clint demanded.

Monica and Jason laughed.

"It is a time machine, son. I probably sent something back a few minutes to prove to you that it worked."

"Something or someone?" Monica asked.

"I don't think you're supposed to see yourself from another timeline. It creates some kind of paradox," Jason added.

"Well, I don't know if I believe all that," Mr. Bower said. "Though, I think it would be quite the shock to the system if it were to happen unexpectedly. And there's no sense is testing that theory if we don't have to, is there."

The machine stopped whirling. It appeared empty. Everyone stared at it, waiting for something to happen. The inventor walked around them and bent over into the machine. When he turned around, there was a black velvet box in his hand.

"Where did you get that?" Clint reached into his coat pocket and pulled out an identical box.

"It was in the time machine," the father answered. "What is it?"

"This is a tennis bracelet I bought for Amanda." Clint opened the box and showed them all. "I was going to give it to her at dinner tonight."

Andrew opened his box. It contained an identical piece of jewelry. Monica took it from him to admire it. She whistled as she held the diamonds up to the light.

"You didn't know I had this," Clint said. "I haven't seen you since I bought it."

"You're right. I had no idea it was in your pocket."

"Then how did you do it?" Clint asked.

"I sent it back in time."

The inventor went over to his machine and started preparing it for the short trip it had just took. They all followed him over and looked at the machine. Monica fiddled with the magnet, while Jason looked at the batteries.

"Marine batteries are enough to power this?"

"This isn't a rail gun." Andrew spoke while still working

on the computer. "I'm not launching something at Mach five. I just need enough current to spin the magnets."

Clint had done three laps around the machine, in awe. Then he went over to the work bench and stared at the computer screen. "You really went back in time."

"That's what I've been trying to tell you," the father said while typing.

"So, the reason you missed the party..."

With a sigh, the older man stopped what he was doing, and turned his full attention to his son. "Is because I didn't know there was a party, or where it was. That was the night I returned to this time, and nothing was how I had left it."

"You don't know what a relief this is. Just when I had decided to follow Mom and your example and get married, you permanently move up here to the lake house, and stop talking to Mom. I thought it was a sign I was making a mistake. Knowing this had nothing to do with me, reassures me that I am doing the right thing."

Looking like fifty pounds had been take off his shoulders, Clint turned around to the other two. "So, how did you guys remember what happened before?".

"We used hypnosis to jog the memories," Jason answered.

"I only remember the old time-line," the father admitted. "That's why I've seemed so confused."

Monica was too shocked to speak. Clint had been second guessing his relationship, and somehow, they convinced him it was a good idea. She wanted to scream with frustration. Unfortunately, no one else seemed concerned. The conversation rolled on without her.

"So, am I next?" Clint asked. "When do I get hypnotized?"

"I don't think that's a good idea." Mr. Bower interrupted. "I think your position in the company is too important to risk your memories being messed with. We need you to be firmly anchored in this time line. Too many people have had undesirable consequences from this already, I don't want to risk you any more than we already have."

Monica sank down on an equipment box. It seemed all hope was lost. She stared down at her feet; the head lamp putting them in a spotlight. Her sneakers were starting to fray, she would need to buy a new pair soon. That would mean another quick trip into Polson for more clothes. That was more than she wanted to think about, so she focused on the dark rock under her feet. She expected Jason to come over and console her, but it was a wrinkled hand that patted hers. "Don't give up. I'm sure we will be able to put everything back the way it was supposed to be."

CHAPTER NINETEEN

Sitting at the small desk in her room, Monica had her laptop in front of her and was typing as fast as she could. After getting down all the details they had gleamed from that afternoon's hypnosis, she leaned back in the chair. Jason stood in the doorway, and she had no idea how long he had been standing there.

"I'd hoped that you hadn't morphed into the person you used to be, wanting to work all evening instead of doing something fun."

"You had me pegged, even down to the glass of wine." She lifted the dark red drink in emphasis before taking a sip. "I would think it'd be in your best interest to put in some extra hours, also. The sooner we get the company back where it's supposed to be, the sooner you can be a globe-trotting playboy again."

"Sacrifice one Friday night to ensure the future ones can be all about fun and not about work?"

"Exactly." She smiled.

"Well, if you think I should." He picked up the satchel laying at his feet. "I was just headed down to the dining room, so I can spread out and get everything organized."

Their work in less-than-lethal weapons covered a wide range of products. Jason had sketched everything he remembered from the other timeline. Some of the drawing looked like artistic rendering while others looked like blueprints. The table was the only thing large enough in the house for him to lay out all the different prototypes.

"Have you done the designs for the riot shield?"

"Um, yes." He dug through his papers until he found the right one, and then handed it to her.

"Thanks, I wanted to look these over." She set them down next to her computer.

"I've been thinking we could expand the market for those. The whole premise behind it is the front of the shield emits light patterns that are disorientating to the eye, forcing people to look away from it." Jason said.

"If you can't look at something, then you can't aim to throw a rock at them,"

"Or shoot a gun?" Jason added.

She nodded in agreement.

"I think the light array could just as easily be placed on a building, giving whatever's inside a first line of defense from being shot at."

"I thought of that," she responded. "I worried that the light array would be like a billboard marking whatever was behind it as a high value target. A man, or a group of men, moving with it would effectively be protected, but I don't think it would work for a large, stationary object. I think people would find a way to aim at it, even if they couldn't look directly at it."

"That sounds like a challenge. I think we're going to have to have a day of testing," he replied, already lost in thoughts of how to set up the experiment.

Monica smiled. "Do you think the paint ball guns are still in the garage?"

"If they're not, then we will have to order some."

Jason went back to the door.

"There is something I wanted to talk to you about," she spoke before he left. "Along with the details about the work we used to do, I've remembered a lot of time working with your father."

"I've noticed the same thing." Jason had turned around at

the threshold. "It seems Rick and I were side by side during a lot of the projects. I didn't want to bring it up, because I didn't want to dredge up the negative stuff we now associate with him."

"It seems we both got along better with our father's business partner than our own Dad. I'm glad I didn't remember any of the old timeline before I met Heath in this one; we had a real connection in the other life. I spent a lot of time in his office learning the ropes from him. If I had gone into his house and tried talking to him the way the other me did, that whole scene in his study would have gone even worse. He would not appreciate me being familiar with him."

Jason laughed. "He is a man that enjoys reverence from others, especially when he first meets someone."

"It's hard to comprehend it's the same man in both timelines. He's so gruff and standoffish. When the merger happened, he was still driven and blunt, he just didn't seem so alone. I wonder if we need to add him to our list of things we need to fix from the other timeline. Do you think he might decide to join the companies after all, if he sees you're working with us?"

"No." Jason raised his hand up, then took a deep breath and lowered it again. "The reason I got sent off to military school was because I tried to change them. I thought they should be like my friend's parents, and the people I saw on television. It was years before I realized the characters on sitcoms are fictional. It was even longer before I understood I was only seeing brief glimpses of my friend's families under ideal conditions when everyone was on their best behavior because visitors were there. My father and I never bonded in either timeline. He's very detail oriented and rarely looks up to see what the big picture is, and having a son that wants to draw instead of crunch numbers is a disappointment for him. I don't think he's really all that different, it's just in the other timeline you were part of his inner circle, while in this one you're a stranger. I have given it some thought and I don't think the fact they were more social in the other timeline means they were happier. I think peer pressure from Andrew, Mimi, Rick and Stephanie forced them to interact more, but I don't think they really enjoyed doing it."

"They actually like their lives?"

"I don't understand it either, but they fight very hard to keep their lives just like they are."

She looked back at her computer screen, shaking her head at the new revelation. "I guess I just really wanted things to be like they were before." She took a deep breath.

"We change what we can, and then we will have to accept what we can't." Jason flashed a smiled and then headed out the door.

The downstairs was quiet and dark. He walked past all the light switches until he was in the dining room. The table was big enough to sit twelve. He didn't need quite that much room, but did take up more than half of it. He circled the room multiple times sorting all the drawings into organized groups.

Next to the last page was the drawing for the Skunk Bombs. Seeing the sketch made him remember more details, so he grabbed a pencil out of his bag, sat down in the closest chair and filled in the missing data.

The sound of the back door drew his thoughts from the diagram in front of him. The swinging kitchen door smacked the wall, and then two sets of footsteps could be heard. Clint was the first to be seen. He kept his eyes forward, head down, and a quick steady pace. Amanda didn't follow his example; her head swiveled, looking into the room she passed. She jerked in surprise at someone else being there.

"What do we have here?"

"This is what I was trying to explain on the way up here," Clint said, stepping back into the framed archway. "Dad hired a couple of assistants, and they are staying here at the house because of the long hours they are putting in."

"I thought you were exaggerating when you said they moved in. Is it normal for your father to bring strangers into the house? I don't know if I want to live like this after we're married." The new fiancé stood with her arms crossed over her bustline, matching her stern expression.

"Like I said," Clint explained. "We have a lot of deadlines looming at work. It's crunch time and my father is using his shop as a place to work without the hustle and bustle of the main office. And they aren't really strangers."

The engaged couple shared a look. It seemed Amanda expected more of an explanation. When she didn't get it, she said. "Well, I hope they are out of this house before summer gets here. I don't want to be trapped in the city with the heat."

"I don't know how long it's going to take," Clint answered.

Amanda didn't retort, and looked unhappy. It was clear she expected to be told everything was going to be all right.

Jason was the one that spoke up. "So, Amanda are you still into S and M?"

There was a moment of silence.

"She's not into that." Clint said.

"What does that have to do with anything?" Amanda asked.

Clint's head whipped to his fiancé when she didn't deny the accusation. "Excuse me?"

"You can't be just vanilla. You're holding back until we're married right?" Amanda asked.

Clint took a step back, with his mouth hung open. It looked like he had to trying moving his mouth a few times before he could get it to form words. "I'll admit I've been holding back from you, but not in the bedroom. I've been hesitant to open up to you, and now I think I know why."

"So, you hired him to investigate me?" Amanda pointed at Jason.

"I'm not a private investigator." Jason said.

"You just happen to know what I like in the bedroom?"

"I'm a member of the Love Tap Club." Jason answered. "I've seen you around there."

"Bullshit." Amanda said.

"Bullshit that you're into that, or bullshit you're a member of the club?" Clint wanted clarification.

"Neither," she responded. "But the only way he would have seen me there was if been in a private suite with me, and I would have remembered him." Her eyes raked his body.

"And when were you going to tell me about this?" Clint asked.

"Our relationship was arranged by our parents while we were in Sunday School. You've always treated me like I'm the same little girl in pig tails. I was waiting for our relationship to get to the adult phase before I address adult desires."

"Did it ever cross your mind that I might not be into that?"

"Yes, it did." She looked at her fiancé and sighed. "If that was the case, then our marriage would be nothing more than a business arrangement, and I would have no problem getting what I needed elsewhere."

"I had you up on a pedestal. To me you've always been that good church girl. I have a hard time imagining you in leather getting whipped."

"She's the one that likes to do the whipping," Jason piped up.

Both of them glared at him. Apparently, no one wanted his input. He put his hands up, not bothering to hide his snickers, and looked back down at the papers in front of him. Amanda huffed and walked away. Clint gave Jason a very unhappy look and then followed her.

After yawning, Monica looked at the bedsides clock; it read three minutes before midnight. She had promised herself that she would go to sleep by ten. Unfortunately, her brain swirled with thoughts, making her unable to do that. Instead of counting sheep, she decided to be productive. But now it was time to really try to get some rest. She closed her laptop, yawning again.

Before she could climb between the sheets, she needed to

get some water. She had to go all the way downstairs to get it. The click of her bedroom door shut out the only light in the hall. She stood with her hand still on the knob, waiting for her eyes to adjust. Jason must already be asleep, because there was no light coming from underneath his door. In the other timeline, there had been night lights in all the hallways. She guessed that hadn't been necessary without kids running around.

Her eyes adjusted enough to see the staircase, and by the time she made her way to the light switch she realized she no longer needed it. The stairs were where the two wings met, so from this point she knew every step by heart. She placed her hand on the rail, recalling Clint and Jason sliding down it. She never had the nerve to do it herself. Standing there in the dark, she wasn't about to start.

Descending the stairs, she imagined she was the Monica from the original timeline. The house was soon to become hers; a wedding present from Clint's parents. Of course, Jason's bedroom would always be his. It wouldn't be home without his sarcastic remarks. She made it to the bottom step, still lost in those thoughts.

Moonlight drew her to the window. The full moon hoovered just over the treetops, reflecting off of the lake. Ripples in the water's surface distorted the image, stretching out the line of light all the way to the shoreline. It was so beautiful, she wanted to just stand there and look at it the rest of the night, but the hardwood floors were cool beneath her feet.

With a sigh, she reminded herself that she lived in the house again. There would be plenty of nights with full moons, and once she had a pair of slippers she would be able to really enjoy it. She turned around to head to the kitchen at the other end of the main hallway. She wasn't expecting the light under that door.

She raised her hand to push open the door, but couldn't bring herself to do it. She was probably being silly. Most likely, it was Andrew or Jason just getting water like she was. With that image in her head, she felt like she was being foolish and pushed the door open.

The bright lights made her blink. She had to look down at the floor while her pupils constricted. When she finally looked up, Clint stood on the other side of the island with all the making of a salami sandwich spread out in front of him. He wore flannel pajamas and a matching robe. She had on a tee-shirt and yoga pants she had just picked up from Walmart. Everything she currently had to wear came from there, until she had time to get back to her apartment. Clint looked over her attire, and didn't seem impressed with what he saw. The cordial greeting she had been just about to say died on her lips. She stepped into the room letting the door swing close behind her.

"Would you like something to eat?"

She glanced up to see him motion to the spread in front of him. "No, thank you. I'm just thirsty."

"There's bottled water in the fridge."

Unable to stop the smirk, she turned around with a bottle of water she had grabbed out of the pantry. "I prefer it room temperature."

"I guess you know where everything is." He went back to spreading mustard on a piece of bread.

"Not everything. Tess was the cook in the other timeline, so the kitchen is pretty much the same. Other things are completely different." She was at the door, looking back before she left. "You only eat late at night when you're stressed. Don't forget an antacid, or you'll be up all night with heartburn."

He didn't say anything, but his expression showed his surprise. She stepped through the door, letting it close behind her.

CHAPTER TWENTY

The message on the white board said Tess had gone to the store. Monica added a note underneath that saying that Jason and her wouldn't be home for dinner. The clock on the stove said the time. She checked her watch to make sure it was right.

"Damn it, where is he?"

She had told Jason they needed to leave by one o'clock. She had her jacket on and was ready to go, but instead of leaving, she had to find him. With a gentle push, the door swung open so she could see the length of the hallway. Long red hair drew her eyes to the staircase. The last person she wanted to see was coming downstairs. She stepped backwards and let the door swing shut.

"What else was I supposed to think. Our entire relationship was planned out by our parents at the country club, like it was just another one of their business deals." Amanda said loud enough to hear through the closed door.

"And you were okay with that? Having your life treated like a merger? Having your husband be nothing more than a business partner you live with?" Clint said.

Monica realized they were fighting. She instantly smiled and danced around the room. This was what she had been waiting for.

"My parents are in politics. Their entire marriage is just a means of furthering their careers. So, the only examples of marriages I've seen that haven't ended in divorce is when the couple agrees to be a united front in the public eye, but have their own lives behind closed doors."

"Well, that's not the example I had. My parents kiss each other good bye every morning. They still go out on dates. They support each other, because they genuinely want the other person to be happy. I assumed we would grow into that."

"In thirty years?" Amanda asked.

"Well, I hoped it wouldn't take that long." Clint was no longer yelling.

Monica moved closed to the door to be able to hear them even when they weren't raising their voices. She knew it was rude to listen. This was something just between the two of them, and not something she needed to be a part of. Still she hovered with her ear inches from the door.

"So, we both just assumed our lives would just be a continuation of what we grew up with, and never bothered to actually get to know the other person."

"Well, I think I've tried."

"Oh, you do, do you?" The red head retorted. "If you think you know me so well, why do you keep buying me diamonds? I get that it's tradition to have one in the engagement ring, and you're a very traditional sort of guy. But it's the only stone you've bought me. You see the other jewelry I wear; it all has color. I've tried dropping hints, pointing out emeralds, garnets, and sapphires when we've been out shopping, but every box I open from you has diamonds."

"I, uh." Clint stammered.

Monica hoped they were going out the other way, but as their voices grew closer, she feared they were going out through the garage. She didn't want to be standing there when they opened the door. Running out of time and options, she ducked into the pantry quietly closing the door behind her.

"I think we both need a little space here to figure things out. I'm headed back to the city… alone." Amanda's voice grew louder as she stormed through the kitchen.

There was the sound of slamming doors, and then nothing else. Had Clint followed her into the garage or was he standing on the other side of the pantry door. She didn't want to open it and find out. What if he opened it? She reached down and grabbed a bottle of water, so at least she would have an excuse for being in there.

She reached out to the door knob, thinking enough time had passed for the coast to be clear, but just before she touched it, the knob turned and pulled away from her.

"Oh, there you are." Jason said, taking the bottle of water from her. "Are you ready to go?"

Rolling her eyes, she picked up another water and followed him out. She looked around the room, half expecting someone else to be there, but she didn't see anyone in the kitchen or out in the garage. They went out the side door, and got in Jason's car. She clicked her seatbelt, and realized he wasn't starting the engine.

"Give me your hand."

"Why?" She looked at him sideways, but didn't move.

"Because I have something for you."

Not sure if it was a prank, she tentatively held out her left hand. She was shocked when he clasped a bracelet around her wrist. When he was done, she moved her arm into the light to see it better.

"Isn't this the tennis bracelet Clint gave Amanda."

"Yep, it was laying in the hallway trash can."

She curled up her lip and moved the jewelry away from her body.

"The can was empty." He paused. Her expression didn't change. "And clean. I promise. I saw them fighting from the stairs. She threw it at him and he threw it into the receptacle."

She stopped scowling, but still held her arm out. "And you think I want a present meant for her."

"I would think you would see it as a sign. He's been buying your favorite jewelry even though she's been pushing him away from it."

Her eyes were locked with Jason's. When she didn't argue with him, he smiled and gave her that you-know-I'm-right look. She rolled her eyes, again, and then brought the gems back into the light to get another look. Did this mean she was the one Clint was actually in love with? Did she dare hope that things would actually work out between them? While she continued to stare at the line of diamonds, Jason started the car and pulled out of the driveway.

❖ ❖ ❖

Smiling, Monica looked up at her childhood home. She had a thousand memories of coming through the front gate. That was the timeline she remembered; riding her bike to school, her mother grading papers at the small desk in the corner of the living room. Technically, Andrew had gone back and changed the timeline only two weeks before. So, had she only lived fourteen days in this life? Which one was the real one? After undergoing hypnosis, she felt like she had lived both lives. Her mother's house was picture perfect, down to the white picket fence. The tulips along the sidewalk were beginning to bloom. This small house, with the covered porch, would always be home. Jason stood beside her, giving her time to be nostalgic.

"Thank you for doing this. She's going to have a hard-enough time hearing I've quit my job and moved away. I don't want to add that I lied about having a boyfriend."

"Technically, you didn't." Jason nudged her elbow. "You had just met me and we were trying to figure out what our relationship was. We could have, in fact, been cousins. She was the one that jumped to the conclusion you were romantically interested in me."

She shook her head. "I knew she was getting the wrong idea, and intentionally let her. So, it is a lie on my part. I would just tell her that we broke up, but I could use your help getting through today."

"So, how long do you plan to pretend?"

"It's only one dinner."

He leaned down and whispered, "What I mean is when are you going to pursue the real boyfriend?"

Dragging her toe along the seam in the concrete, she stared at the ground. "I don't know if I ever will. I'm not the same person I was in the first timeline."

"Yes, you are."

"No, I'm not." She looked him in the eye. "No matter how many memories I recover, I still have all the memories from this one. I'm middle class. I'm blue jeans, and public schools, and playing charades with my family."

"I think, underneath all that, you will find there is still a bond between you two."

"Well, we're not digging into that tonight. For the next few hours, I need you to pretend you are my one and only."

"Okay," He said with a nod. Then with a huge smile, he pulled her into a tight embrace and whispered in her ear. "So, how much of a show do you want me to put on?"

She rolled her eyes and pushed him away. "None. I don't like public displays of affection with men I really am dating, let alone men I'm just pretending to."

After smoothing out the wrinkles he'd put in her dress, she looked up to see her mother watching them through the living room window. *Great.* She rolled her eyes. The glowing smile on the older woman's face told Monica she was already convinced of the relationship. Taking Jason by the shirt sleeve, she pulled him towards the steps.

"Happy Birthday!" her stepfather, Paul Meyers, yelled as soon as he opened the door.

"Yes, happy birthday, dear." Her mother walked up and gave her a big hug. The embrace felt good, and reassured her that she had made the right decision to keep everything from her mom. This house was her safe haven, and it didn't need to be disturbed. Announcing that she believed in an alternate timeline would just cause a rift between them. She wasn't willing to risk that, because with everything going on, she needed her mother.

"Um, this is my friend, Jason."

Her parents exchanged a look like they were humoring her by letting her call him just a friend.

"I'm sorry we're late…"

Paul interrupted her excuse. "Oh, you're fine. Dinner is just coming out of the oven, so you're right on time." Then he turned to the new house guest. "Welcome. We're glad you could join us."

The kitchen timer buzzed. "Oh, we better get that." Both parents left the room.

"We have a tradition of family dinners on our birthdays."

"No wonder they looked at me like that, bring me home for a dinner that supposed to be just family."

"Oh, don't be silly. I've always invited a friend over. I just had to plan my party on another night, so this night could be special." She led him into the dinning room. "And the birthday person isn't allowed to lift a finger to help."

It was ironic, all the rituals to celebrate getting older actually made her feel like she was a kid again. All dinners were eaten at this table, but holidays were always occasions to celebrate. Easter hams, thanksgiving turkeys, even the deserts were always traditional. The only thing better than the food was the unconditional love that always filled the house. She sat down at the head of the table, knowing it was expected since it was her day. Jason sat down across from her.

Jason didn't say anything, but he looked around the room. She looked around too, wondering what he thought of their surroundings. The window looked out at a lilac bush. The bright green leaves of spring had just unfurled, and it would be a few weeks before the flowers erupted. She made a mental note to come back and pick some for her bedroom. She couldn't see it from her chair, but there was a pastel painting of a cottage with flowers hanging on the wall behind her. It wasn't by anyone famous or worth a lot of money, but she thought it made the room. Would her friend agree? She really couldn't tell much from his blank expression. The china hutch stood across from the window. The glass door revealed almost empty shelves, since most of the contents were on the table. It hadn't been brought out just because she had brought a guest. The good china was used on all holidays and birthdays.

The bang of the opening door interrupted her thoughts. A large pan of lasagna was brought out, followed by a loaf of garlic bread and a large bowl of salad. It was set in the middle of the table. Her parents sat down in the empty seats, and dishes were passed around until the plates were filled with food.

"So, what's up with my favorite accountant?" Paul asked.

"Funny you should ask, I'm not an accountant anymore."

Mrs. Meyers dropped her fork. The sound of it hitting her plate rang out in the silence. Jason was the only one not staring at her in shock, he kept his head down and shoveled in food.

"What do you mean, honey?" Stephanie asked in that calm motherly tone that meant she was trying really hard to keep her cool.

She hadn't expected her mom to react like that. To be honest, she had never disappointed her mother before. She had always been the good girl. She never came home drunk, reeking of cigarette smoke. This was the first time she ever made a decision without thoroughly discussing it with her parents.

"I stumbled into an exciting new position." Monica paused, hoping she wouldn't have to get into all the details. But the expectant looks on both her parent's faces told her she needed to keep going. "I'm proofing mathematical equations for a less-than-lethal weapons manufacturer."

"That sounds stimulating, but it doesn't seem like a job that would last very long. What do you plan to do when they don't need you anymore?" Stephanie asked in the tone she used when she wasn't happy. Next would come a rational list of reasons why this wasn't a good idea.

"Well, I don't think that's going to be a problem. I have about a year's worth of work piled up in my in-box, right now. Even it doesn't work out, I can always go back to accounting."

"Your father did that kind of work. You aren't like him.

160

You don't have the drive to make profit. You're not going to be happy trying to do the same thing he did."

"Mom, I'm not him and I'm not you. I can't spend all day in a room with thirty kids. I like being isolated, with just a couple co-workers. I went into accounting so I could work independently. That part's been great, but I'm bored out of my mind with the actual job. Here I have the best of both worlds. I get to work with a small team, and I'm challenged by what I do."

"What's the name of the company?" her mother asked, and then took a small bite.

"Crowne, Inc."

The older woman flinched, but covered it up by wiping the corners of her mouth with her napkin. She kept her face serene and didn't say anything about recognizing the name of the company. "Did they say what drew them to you?"

"It was a chance meeting." This was the part she didn't want to do; she had lie to her mother. Once the lie was out of her mouth, she would be saddled with it the rest of her life. With that in mind, she tried to keep as close to the truth as she could. "They didn't come to me. Jason and I were doing a scavenger hunt and ran into Mr. Bower. He was struggling with an equation, so I purposed that I would help him with it if he would help us. He was so impressed when I solved it, he offered me a job on the spot."

Paul looked like the proud papa, smiling at her. He had gone back to eating his own dinner. Monica took a bite of her own, savoring her mother's delicious cooking. It was still the best lasagna she had eaten, in either timeline.

"Mom, I know you're worried about me, but you don't need to be. I don't have stars in my eyes. I haven't been happy bookkeeping. Now I get to do something that not only excites me, but also challenges me. Never before have I felt accomplished at the end of the day. For the first time I have more than just a job. I make a difference in the world. The products I make will save someone's life."

"I can see how happy this has made you." Stephanie patted her daughter's hand. "I assumed that was due to your new *friendship*, but now I see it's more than that."

"It's been a busy couple of weeks, but you don't need to worry that I'm getting caught up in a tidal wave. Well, maybe I am a little bit, but I assure you I'm keeping my head above water."

"It sounds like we have a lot of things to celebrate," Paul said.

That had gone better than she thought it would. She just started to relax, thinking they had discussed everything she thought had land mines.

"So, Jason, what do you do for a living?"

"He's in the Air Force." Monica answered for him, hoping the intense stare she gave him made him understand not to bring up his connection with her new job. If they found out his last name, her mother would instantly know who he was, especially since then had recently been dredging all the memories of the past. He gave her a reassuring smile before he started talking.

"I just transferred to the Base here. I met Monica while I was changing my address at the bank. She's been great about showing me around town."

Paul reached across the table to get another slice of lasagna.

"Make sure you save room for dessert." His wife stopped him. "There is a birthday cake and ice cream in there."

Her stepfather put down the spatula and sat back in his chair with his hands folded over his stomach.

"Is it my favorite?" the daughter asked.

"Of course. Unless that something else that has changed?"

"Nope. I will always want marble cake."

"Do you want any help getting that?" Jason asked.

"No, thank you." Stephanie smiled at the younger man. "It's your first time here, so you are company. Enjoy it while it lasts. Before you know it, I'll expect you to pitch in."

The parents got up and went into the kitchen, carrying

some of the dinner dishes that were no longer needed. When the door closed, Jason said. "See, you didn't need me here. You had everything under control."

"It was still reassuring to have you around."

Paul came out carrying a double layered cake covered in chocolate frosting. Lit candles circled the top. It was placed in front of Monica, where her dinner plate had just been. Stephanie was right behind him with the ice cream and serving dishes. Once everyone sat down, they all sang 'Happy birthday', and then looked at her expectantly when they were done. She stared into the flames, knowing they were waiting for her to make a wish. So many good things had happened, did she dare hope for more? It was her birthday, and it wasn't like anyone would know what she wished for. With Clint's image firmly in her mind, she drew in a deep breath, and then blew out all the candles in one try.

"So, what's your intentions with our daughter?" Paul asked out of the blue.

Monica felt like her eyes were going to pop out of her head, but Jason didn't look ruffled in the slightest. In fact, he looked like he'd been waiting for it.

"She's one the most amazing people I know. I won't let her out of my life."

Paul looked pleasantly surprised by the answer and Stephanie looked blown away by it. Jason sat with his eyes locked on the young lady across the table from him, which happened to be the only person that knew that the grin turning up the corners of his mouth meant he thought his answer was a funny joke.

CHAPTER
TWENTY-ONE

The water in her bottle was still cold, and felt good on Monica's dry throat. She looked around the shop, assessing what she had done so far. There were no longer food wrappers and empty cans on the tables. She had put most of the tools away, only leaving out what they were still using.

"I just got off the phone with the tool and die shop," Clint said loudly so his father could hear it on the other side of the building. "They have the steel molds done, and have started making the plastic parts. We just have to pick them up next week."

"That's good to hear."

They were all working as a team again, and getting things accomplished. Monica had come to the front desk to sit down and take a break. Not able to completely stop, she read over the equations on the white board. It was a great place to work out problems, because errors could easily be erased. Sometimes she would leave problems on the board for hours or even days so she could randomly look at them with fresh eyes. Only when she was sure she had analyzed each part of it from every angle did she write it down else where. She realized everything on the board had already been confirmed and copied into the computer. She stood up, grabbed the eraser.

Clint grabbed her wrist as she swiped across the top. "What is this?"

She stared at her hand and the eraser in it, trying to figure out what he was upset about. Nothing seemed out of place to her. Clint lowered her arm, but still kept hold.

"Did you think you could steal this and no one would notice?"

She thought he was talking about the eraser, and was about to say that she had just picked it up when the light glinted off the tennis bracelet. She had completely forgot she was wearing it. She imagined he did want to know where she had got it from.

"I gave it to her," Jason said. Making both of them jump in surprise. He stood right behind them. Clint dropped her arm as he turned around.

"You *gave* it to her?" Clint's voice rose. He turned and watched his father approach. "You brought thieves into our house."

"You threw it in the trash can."

"I was just making a point by throwing it in the receptacle. I had full intentions of retrieving it later."

"All I did was help you get it to the person that was meant to have it."

Clint looked around at everyone. "What does that mean?"

"In the other timeline…"

"I thought I was only supposed to know what happens in this time." Clint interrupted.

Andrew stepped forward to stand in front of his son. "In the other timeline, you were engaged just like in this one. Except it was Monica you were supposed to marry."

"She's the one that likes diamonds." Jason added.

This was the moment Monica had been worried about. Would he laugh at the idea? Would he suddenly remember and pull her into a kiss? Uncertain, she held her breath until he turned and looked at her. His face was neutral; not giving her any hints as to what he was thinking.

"Oh, thank god." Clint's shoulder's sagged as he let out a pent-up breath. "I thought Amanda had changed when I put the ring on her finger. Overnight, I suddenly couldn't say or do the right thing. I tried to make up for whatever I had done wrong by taking her for a walk along the river front..."

"By the statue of the bear?" Monica asked.

"Yes."

"The one we stopped at right after our first kiss, when we had just admitted our feelings for each other, and we couldn't wait to get back to your apartment. You pulled me across the grass, leaned up against the stone base and leaned into me. We made out until we noticed all of the office employees staring at us from their windows."

"I took Amanda there; all she said was that the bear looked goofy. Then she pointed out a bag of dog poop at the edge of the grass and refused to step off the pavement."

"There is no way I would let dog poop, bagged or a steaming fresh pile, keep me from recreating that moment. Just go to the other side of the statue."

Clint laughed and took her hand in his. "That's how I felt. I was lost when she couldn't care less about it. All she wanted to do was go over to the carrousel."

"With all the screaming kids?"

"Exactly!" Clint raised his hand in emphasis.

She pressed her cheek to his and whispered into his ear. "You haven't been doing all the wrong things. You've been doing all the right things with the wrong woman." When she stepped back, he was staring at their joined hands.

"I was so excited when I found this in the store. I thought it was perfect. It was so disheartening when Amanda didn't like it."

"I think it's stunning."

Clint looked up and met her eyes. She smiled. He searched her face. She knew exactly what he was looking for; acceptance. His had slid down her wrist, until his fingers intertwined with hers. Her skin warmed with the contact. Without saying anything, Jason and Andrew turned around and went back to work. Monica closed her eyes and took a second to enjoy Clint's hand touching hers. When she opened her eyes, he was looking down at their hands, his face was relaxed, and his lips were turned up at the corners. It was an expression she hadn't seen in this timeline, and was relieved to.

"Where is the wedding supposed to be?"

"It was going to be at the Paws Up Resort, on June twenty-first."

He led her to the chair. When she sat down in it, he sat down on the desk, still holding her hand. "Why that day?"

"It's the longest day of the year. I always thought we had the kind of love that needed to longest day to celebrate."

"You seem tense."

"I was scared I would never get to touch you like this again. You were engaged to another woman, and when I finally did find you, you didn't know me at all."

"I wanted to." Clint laughed at her surprise. "You randomly show up at my door with another man. You asked me if I knew you, and I answered truthfully when I said I didn't. But I wanted to know you. There's an intensity about you that drew me in. But then I looked over at Jason, and he had the same ardent look. I figured I was misreading things, and needed to leave."

"Then I was scared I was too different than the me from the other timeline. I no longer shop in the most expensive department stores or frequent five-star restaurants."

"Those are just details?"

"Are they?" She looked up and met his eyes. "What are you going to think when I save plastic containers that food comes in to use as Tupperware, so I don't have to feel guilty about throwing it away if I forgot about it in the fridge and the food got moldy."

"Tell me about us. How did we fall in love?"

"For as long as I can remember, both Jason and you were a part of my life. At first, it was just on Thursday's evening, and then on holidays and during the summer, and finally every weekend. I think I was in middle school when I noticed I reacted differently to the two of you. Jason was always my friend, and I was always happy to see him. I was happy to see you too, but with you I worried about how I worded things. I was scared you weren't going to take it right. I got so flustered; I wouldn't speak. Since I was relaxed around Jason, you assumed I liked him more. You gave me the cold shoulder. It wasn't until college we had a chance to hang out, just the two of us. Pretty quickly, we were together every day. Once we finally admitted our feelings for each other, we were inseparable.

"Then one day I woke up reaching for you, and you weren't there. It was like, suddenly you didn't exist. I wasn't even the same person. I was gloomy and depressed. So, when I did find you and you didn't respond to me, I assumed it was because I had changed too much. I didn't think you could love the new me."

Clint raised her hand up. "For the last two weeks, my relationship with Amanda has been frustrating. I never feel like I'm good enough, and she doesn't act like the girl I grew up with. I think my memories were too strong for time to erase, so it just put someone in that spot. I want the woman I remember. I want you." He kissed her hand.

The sound of a clearing throat drew their attention away from each other and to the person on the other side of the desk. Monica pulled her hand back when she saw Amanda standing there. Neither of them had heard her come in.

"I can't marry you." Clint jumped up.

"No shit." Amanda retorted.

Motion made Monica look over Amanda's shoulder. Jason carried up parts from the back. As soon as he saw who was standing there, he stopped and quietly put down what was in his hands on the nearest table. She thought he would leave, but he watched the scene, instead.

"I'm sorry." Clint stepped forward.

The redhead put her hand up to stop him. "I've never seen

this side of you. I didn't think you were the romantic type. Now I see, if you're with the right woman, you are. Seeing this confirms we don't belong together."

"I never meant for any of this to happen."

"I know you didn't." She gave him a reassuring smile. "That's not why I came here. I have to know if I'm walking away from just you, or my position with the company, also."

"Would you like to keep your job?" Clint sounded surprised.

"That's what I've been thinking about, and I'm not sure. I have a few questions before I make a decision. Nothing's happened in production in the year I've interned here, and suddenly you've produced five new items in a week. And all of this has been done out in your shed instead of in our state-of-the-art lab. Before I'm past the point of no return, I want to know what's going on here. Then I will decide if I'm going to stay."

"We've brought in new people with new ideas, you're seeing the fruits of that."

"You expect me to believe that? You can sell that line to people outside the company, but I've seen a little too much to buy it. You father is having some kind of breakdown. You've been overwhelmed with running the show. And two new assistants magically make everything better and suddenly do a years' worth of work? What's really going on here?"

"Have you heard of alternative time lines?" Jason stepped forward and asked.

"Like from sci-fi movies?" She turned to him, looking like she was trying to understand the sudden subject change.

"Exactly," He was pleased she got the reference. "There was another time line where Clint, Monica and I all grew up spending our summers together at the lake house because our fathers were all business partners."

Amanda stared at him for a couple seconds, and then asked, "What's your father's name?"

"Heath Radcliff."

She nodded in acknowledgement she recognized the

name. "And her father?"

"Rick Lane."

"I've never heard of him," Amanda said.

Andrew appeared next to the younger, taller man. He looked displeased with what he overheard, but stayed silent.

"He was my father's business partner. He died twenty years ago."

"But in this other timeline, he didn't die and they merged their company with Andrew's."

"Wow. You're catching on a lot faster than I thought you would."

"Just because I can follow your train of thought doesn't mean I believe what you're saying." Amanda crossed her arms over her chest.

"Thank you for giving me a chance to explain." Jason leaned against a table. "I know it sounds crazy. We were more accepting of it because we were all effected by it... and we saw the time machine."

"So, who was I in the last life?" Amanda turned to Clint.

He didn't know, so he looked to Monica. She shrugged and looked at Andrew. The older man just shook his head. They all turned to Jason.

"You worked for a cosmetic company."

"I sold make-up for a living?"

"It's a well-known company," Jason went on. "You work in international sales, it's really no different than what you do here."

"No one know...How could you...That was years ago?"

"What was years ago?" Clint asked.

"My mother made arrangements with one of her sorority sisters for me to have a job at her cosmetic company. The started talking as soon as I major in international business relations. By my sophomore year, they were ready to draw up my contract. That was when I took interest in Crowne, Inc. If I worked with my fiancé, my mother couldn't interfere with that. I never told anyone about that, and I know my mother wouldn't because she considered it a failure." She faced Jason. "How did you know?"

"In the other time line, you weren't engaged to Clint. Without him, you didn't have a way to avoid the job."

The red head looked shocked. "You're not kidding around. Someone went back in time and stole this stuff?"

"No."

Andrew cleared his throat. "Nothing was stolen. In the old timeline, these were the products we'd manufactured. Going back in time somehow changed that. All the kids have been doing is remembering what was done in the other life, so we can recreate it here."

There was a long pause. No one spoke, just watched as the outsider processed what she had heard.

"Let me see if I understand this." She pointed at Andrew. "You went back in time, stopped the merger, Rick died, and then all this stuff that had been invented suddenly didn't exist. You three remember it all, so you're reinventing your own products?"

"Basically," the old man replied. "I only intended one small change. All the things you listed were unintentional consequences."

"You're taking this very well." Clint said.

"I am, huh. I guess I did think of us as just a business merger, or perhaps as a means to get the job I wanted. Surprisingly, I've even willing to schmooze politicians. I hated being around that as a child. Everyone was so fake. But I really care about what we are doing. I think society will live more harmoniously if the military and police can quell uprisings without resorting to deadly force. Not only here, but around the globe. I wake up in the morning wanting to come to work. I even like seeing you at the office. You do a great job of running the company. With the impending deadlines and your father taking off, we've been consumed by work and able to avoid the things we don't want to talk about."

"Until it all got thrown in our face." Clint said with a

glance to Jason.

"Exactly" The redhead responded.

Amanda paused and then looked at Jason. "So, you knew me?"

"We hooked up."

"Oh, you did know me from the club. Just from a time I don't recall. I'm usually pretty picky about who I connect with." She looked over the man, like she imagined what he looked like naked.

"Well, my selection process was just as stringent as yours."

"How did you both end up back here?" Amanda asked.

"Ends up, Jason and I could remember some things from the other time line." Monica answered her. "And have worked to recover even more memories."

"We are trying to get things back to how they were in the old timeline. Some things are going to be different, but we think we can at least get this company back to where it was before."

"And in this other timeline, you two were a couple." Amanda pointed to Clint and Monica.

Monica spoke up. "We dated for years, and were going to get married this summer."

"And you remembered him, even though your new life was completely different."

"I would wake up reaching for him, and had to remember that he wasn't there."

That seemed to be the last of the questions. Amanda looked around the room, as if seeing it for the first time. From the half-erased equation on the board, to the products all in various stages of assembly, everything around her supported what had been said.

"Have you thought about whether or not you're going to keep your job now that you know about our little secret?" Clint asked.

"Would you like me to stay?"

"I hadn't thought about it until you brought it up a few

minutes ago. I had assumed that if you left me, you would leave the company. But now that I think about it, that's silly. You've worked really hard and contributed a lot. It would be nice if you could stay on with us."

"I think you should stay." Everyone showed their surprise at Jason sharing his opinion. "In the last timeline, I handled all of the overseas marketing by myself. I basically had three sets of parents then, and loved getting out on my own. In this life, I've already been on my own for ten years and am not looking forward to starting a life of even more of it. If we expected to get any new business, besides the contracts we already have, we will need to focus abroad. It would be really nice to have some help with that."

He concluded by giving Amanda a huge smile. She suddenly looked skeptical, when she hadn't before.

"That's Jason being reserved and trying not to flirt." Monica interjected. "He's being sincere in saying that he would like to work with you."

"That wasn't a come on?"

"Why do I even bother to try to not flirt, when I still get accused of doing it? This smile and charm works on the customers. They like it and buy whatever I'm selling. If I'm too much for you, if you don't think you can handle this, maybe you better sell cosmetics."

Her eyes narrowed on Jason. "I can take whatever you dish out." She turned to Clint. "Job accepted." They shook hands.

"So, where is this time machine?" Amanda asked.

"It's…"

"Jason!" Andrew interrupted and put his hand on the younger man's shoulder. "I thought of all people, you'd understand the importance of secrecy on this."

Jason looked down. "You're right. I wasn't thinking. She's been affected by this, so I thought she should know. I guess I got caught up in telling her everything."

"I understand why you wanted to share." Andrew patted the young man on the back. "It's natural to want to. But this conversation has made me realize we're going to need to destroy the time machine."

"Dad, do you really want to do that? You've accomplished what most people consider impossible. Can you just tear it all apart?"

"I will admit, there is a part of me that doesn't want to. It is an amazing achievement. Unfortunately, it can never be used again. We've seen what happens when I went back in time. I fear the results can be just as treacherous if we go into the future. Just bringing back knowledge of what's going to happen would change the timeline, making that future never happen. I can't risk it being used again. I need to make it inoperable."

"What ever you decide. We are here for you."

Mr. Bower looked down at his watch. "We have enough daylight left. We should do it now."

"We're on a deadline for work. Should we stop everything to do this now?"

"We have to. I have to know that I will not be responsible for another death. I see now that only way I can know it's safe is to make sure it is never used again."

Monica went over to the tote filled with spelunking safety gear. "Let's do this."

Amanda's eyes lit up when she found out there was enough gear for her to join them. "I'm so excited. I get to see it."

"You will have to do physical labor if you come down with us," Jason called out.

"I know," she came around the shelves zipping up coveralls. "Ready, willing and able."

Clint and Jason pulled wheeled carts into the mineshaft. Amanda wasn't going to show fear in front of Jason. She walked side by side with him into the dark tunnel.

"So, what was our relationship in this last life?"

"We spent three nights together down in the dungeon." Jason responded.

She smiled at him, then returned her attention to where she walked.

"You're the first person I did multiple sessions with. The whole time I was in London, all I could think about was what you were going to do to me. When I got back, I slipped and told 'the Cleavers' back there that I had a date."

"Is that why you keep staring at me, because you're thinking about the sex?"

"That's part of it, but not all. I love watching you strut into the kitchen with the same confidence you have when you're being a dominatrix. Now, I see it's not the outfit or the props that makes you the center of attention. Even in a summer dress and sandals you are a force to be reckoned with."

She was very quiet, not responding to what he said as they continued deeper into the shaft. Finally, he couldn't take the silent treatment, and prompted her to respond.

"This other me must have been more open," she said. "I always have a mask on, and never let anyone know who I am."

"In that timeline, you weren't engaged. And I wouldn't say you were *open* then. I just happened to be one of the few people you took off your mask for."

"I don't know what that would feel like, to be in a relationship with someone I could be completely open and honest with."

"Me, either." Jason replied.

Monica had fallen into step next to the shorter of the two men. Her fingers brushed against his as they walked. The next thing she knew, they were holding hands. Her skin tingled with the contact. Electricity ran up her arm. This was what she had been missing the last couple weeks. The relief of touching him was quickly overshadowed by a feeling of guilt. Was it fair for her to be touching him like that in front of Amanda? She angled her flashlight up to reveal the redhead walking in front of them. She was lost in conversation with Jason.

"What language are they speaking?" Clint asked.

"I don't think it's Japanese. Chinese maybe?"

The other couple never noticed the light shining on them or that they were being talked about. Monica lowered the beam so the ground in front of them was illuminated. Then she squeezed her fiancé's hand, and just enjoyed the close proximity to him.

The first time they made the trip, it had seemed like a lot of time passed before the dark tunnels revealed the destination. This time it felt like they had only been hiking a few minutes when the steel structure loomed up in front of them.

"This is it?" Amanda shined her flashlight on the metallic rings. "Does it really work?"

"Well, you know that bracelet you threw away?" Jason asked. "It took a little trip through time."

"I thought *Andrew* used the time machine."

"I did, sweetie. I just sent the trinket through to prove that it worked." Mr. Bower had been the last in line. He stepped around them to approach the time machine. Everyone was silent as he ran his hands over the rails. The old man's head hung down. No one else moved until he did.

"Okay. This wiring is expensive, so we need to salvage it."

"What about the metal frame, are we going to recycle it?" Clint asked.

"No. I can't risk anyone else seeing the design. I have plan for that."

Amanda was not familiar with the machinery or the tools, so she stayed close to Jason following his instructions to help him dismantle the magnets.

"So, who was I dating to in this other life?"

"Nobody, as far as I know." Jason coiled up wire on her outstretched arm. "We didn't do a lot of talking when we were together, but we are in the same gossip circles and I hadn't heard anything."

"I find it hard to believe my mother wouldn't have arranged something, in whatever timeline."

"I'm pretty sure she tried, it just didn't work out like it did with Clint, in this timeline. Rumor was you had already been pushed into things you didn't want to do, so you refused your mother's advice on who to marry."

"I can see being stuck in a job I don't like, I wouldn't be in a rush to let her interfere with the rest of my life."

"Both jobs were international sales, I don't see what the big difference is." Jason said. "You obviously use cosmetics."

"I use toilet paper, too. That doesn't mean I want to spend my whole life selling it."

By the time they were done, the machine looked like nothing more than a skeleton. The long electrical cords that ran all the way into the mine had been disconnected, rolled up and taken to the shop. A single red cord was put in its place. The only thing left not welded to the frame was the laptop, with Andrew carried over and set on the platform in the middle on the time machine.

"What are you doing, Dad?"

"All of my notes, the blueprints, and the mathematical equations are all on that computer. It must be destroyed."

With a deep sigh, the old man turned around and led them out. They were all dirty and covered in sweat by the time they gathered around the mine entrance.

"Aren't explosives like these illegal?" Amanda asked.

"I have a license for them" Andrew said.

"Does your license cover using them on private property to implode a mine?" Monica asked.

"No. The license if for industrial applications. But this is one of those situations where forgiveness is easier than permission. Besides, it's just going to be one blast. It will be over before anyone realizes what happened."

The blast barricade they used for testing products was set up where the detonator cord ended. The space was designed for two men, but they all squeezed behind the bullet proof glass so they could see what was happening.

"Okay, everyone. Hearing protection on. This is going to be loud."

Andrew pressed the red button. The blast wave smacked the barricade with enough force to push the thick steel frame back four inches. The rush of air had all their hair standing on end. When they looked up, the huge dust cloud was still settling over the crater.

"All right, let's get all this debris cleaned up. Non-explosive plastic tubing would be a give away that it wasn't a natural cave in if the police show up."

Jason, Monica and Amanda started cleaning the up mess. Andrew leaned down to do the same, but Clint grabbed him before he could.

"Hey Dad, I told Mom the wedding is off, that you were right. Why don't you go into the city and see her?"

"I would love to, there's just one problem. I don't know the address?"

"What do you mean you don't know where we live?"

"It seems we have a different house in this timeline than we did in the last. I went to the place on Kona Ranch Road, and no one there knew me. It was quite embarrassing."

Clint laughed. "I imagine it was." He pulled his Dad into a hug. "No worries. I'll put the address in your GPS. We'll get you there."

The End

Visit C.E.Chester on Facebook.

Made in the USA
Monee, IL
30 September 2020